Hiccup Horrendous Haddock the Third was an awesome swordfighter, a dragon whisperer, and the greatest Viking Hero who ever lived. But Hiccup's memoirs look back to when he was a very ordinary boy who found it hard to be a hero.

You don't *have* to read the Hiccup memoirs in order. But if you want to, this is the right order:

**A big thank you to Simon Cowell, Tina Jalava and
Andrea Malaskova for all their hard work and support.**

Little, Brown and Company

Hachette Book Group
1290 Avenue of the Americas, New York, NY 10104
Visit us at lb-kids.com

Little, Brown and Company is a division of Hachette Book Group, Inc.
The Little, Brown name and logo are trademarks of Hachette Book Group, Inc.

The publisher is not responsible for websites (or their content) that are not owned by the publisher.

First U.S. Trade Paperback Edition: February 2010
First U.S. Hardcover Edition: May 2005
First published in Great Britain in 2004 by Hodder Children's Books

Library of Congress Cataloging-in-Publication Data
Cowell, Cressida.
  How to be a pirate / by Hiccup Horrendous Haddock III ; translated from the Old Norse by
Cressida Cowell. — 1st U.S. ed.
    p. cm.
  "First published in Great Britain in 2004 by Hodder Children's Book's — t.p. verso.
  Summery: Follows the further adventures and misadventures of Hiccup Horrendous Haddock
the Third as his Viking training continues and his father leads a stranger and the Hairy Hooligans
to the Isle of Skullions in search of a pirate's treasure.
  ISBN 978-0-316-15598-4 (hc) / 978-0-316-08528-1 (pb)
  1. Vikings — Juvenile fiction. [1. Vikings — Fiction, 2. Pirates —
Fictions. 3. Dragons — Fiction. 4. Buried treasure — Fictions.
5. Humorous stories.] I. Title.
PZ7.C83535H1 2005
[Fic]—dc22

2004048636

25

LSC-C

Printed in the United States of America

How to Be ~a~ Pirate

by Cressida Cowell

LITTLE, BROWN AND COMPANY
New York   Boston

HICCUP the Hero of this Story

TOOTHLESS
Hiccup's disobedient little dragon

Hiccup's best friend
FISHLEGS

STOICK THE VAST
Hiccup's father and Chief of the Hooligan (tough & dim)

HORRORCOW
Fishlegs's dragon

MUM

SNOTLOUT

Top of the class at Bashyball, Advanced Rudery, Senseless Violence and everything else

DOGSBREATH
THE DUHBRAIN
Snotlout's friend + fellow bully

FIREWORM
Snotlout's dragon

ALVIN
a Poor-But-Honest Farmer

GOBBER THE BELCH →
teacher in charge of the Pirate Training Program

REVIEWS FOR
How to Be a Pirate

"Hiccup's scariest, funniest adventure so far."
The Pirate Post

"Just who does this Horrendous Haddock think he is?
Us dragons could have him for breakfast."
The Scaly Mail

~ CONTENTS ~

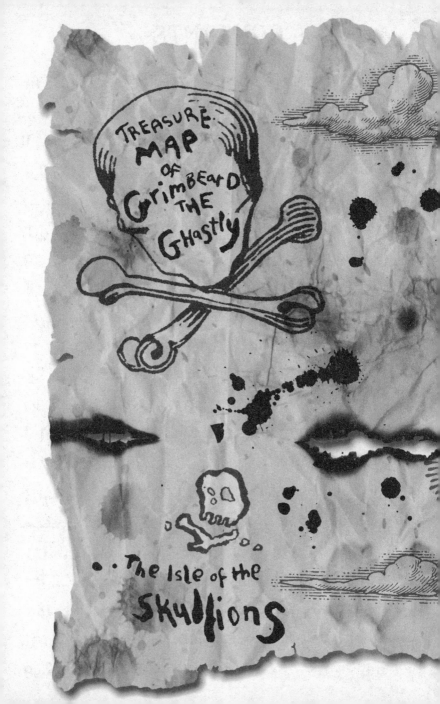

Not to Scale

N
W
E
S

The Outcast Lands

There be
TREASURE
at the
Death's Head.

The
Peaceable
Country

Isle of Berk

Meathead Islands

1. SWORDFIGHTING AT SEA (BEGINNERS ONLY)

Thor was SERIOUSLY annoyed.

He had sent a mighty summer storm to claw up the seas around the bleak little Isle of Berk. A black wind was shrieking across the wild and angry ocean. Furious thunder boomed overhead. Lightning speared into the water.

Only a madman would think it was the kind of weather for a pleasant sail.

But, amazingly, there was *one* ship being hurled violently from wave to wave, the hungry ocean chewing at her sides, hoping to tip her over and swallow the souls aboard and grind their bones into sand.

The madman in charge of this

ship was Gobber the Belch. Gobber ran the Pirate Training Program on the Isle of Berk and this crazy voyage was, in fact, one of Gobber's lessons, Swordfighting at Sea (Beginners Only).

"OKAY, YOU DRIPPY LOT!" yelled Gobber, a six-and-a-half-foot hairy muscle-bound lunatic, with a beard like a ferret having a fit and biceps the size of your head. "PUT YOUR BACKS INTO IT, FOR THOR'S SAKE. YOU ARE NOT AN ICKLE PRETTY JELLYFISH.... HICCUP, YOU ARE ROWING LIKE AN EIGHT-YEAR-OLD.... THE FAT BIT OF THE OAR GOES IN THE WATER.... WE HAVEN'T GOT ALL YEAR TO GET THERE ...," etc. etc.

Hiccup Horrendous Haddock the Third gritted his teeth as a big wave came screaming over the side and hit him full in the face.

Hiccup is, in fact, the Hero of this story, although you would never have guessed this to look at him. He was on the small side and had the sort of face that was almost entirely unmemorable.

There were twelve other boys struggling with the oars of that ship, and practically all of them looked more like Viking Heroes than Hiccup did.

Wartihog, for instance, was only eleven, but he already had a fine crop of bubbling adolescent pimples and a personal odor problem. Dogsbreath could row as hard as anybody else with one hand, while picking his nose with the other. Snotlout was a natural leader. Clueless had ear hair.

Hiccup was just absolutely average, the kind of unremarkable, skinny, freckled boy who was easy to overlook in a crowd.

Beneath the rowing benches, thirteen dragons were huddled, one for each boy.

The dragon belonging to Hiccup was much, much smaller than the others. His name was Toothless, an emerald green Common or Garden dragon with enormous eyes and a sulky expression.

He was whining to Hiccup in Dragonese.*

"These Vikings c-c-crazy. Toothless g-g-got salt in his wings. Toothless sitting in a big cold puddle. Toothless h-h-hungry.... F-F-FEED ME." He tugged at Hiccup's pants. "Toothless need f-f-food NOW."

a dragon's wings make a great umbrella...

---

* Dragonese was the native tongue of the dragons. I have translated it into English for the benefit of those readers whose Dragonese is a bit rusty. Only Hiccup could understand this fascinating language.

"I'm sorry, Toothless." Hiccup winced as the boat plunged maniacally downwards on the back of another monstrous wave. "But this is not a good moment. . . ."

"THOR ONLY KNOWS," yelled Gobber, "how you USELESS LOT got initiated into the tribe of the Hairy Hooligans . . . but you now face four tough years on the Pirate Training Program before you can truly call yourselves VIKINGS."

"Oh great," thought Hiccup gloomily.

"We will begin with the most important Viking Skill of all . . . SWORDFIGHTING AT SEA." Gobber grinned.

"The rules of Pirate Swordfighting are . . . THERE ARE NO RULES. In this lesson, biting, gouging, scratching and anything else particularly nasty all get you extra points. The first boy to call out 'I submit' shall be the loser."

"Or we all drown," muttered Hiccup, "whichever is the sooner."

"NOW," shouted Gobber. "I NOMINATE THE FIRST BOY AS DOGSBREATH THE DUHBRAIN. WHO'S GOING TO FIGHT HIM?"

Dogsbreath the Duhbrain grunted happily at the thought of spilling blood. Dogsbreath was a mindless thug of a boy with hairy knuckles that practically grazed the ground as he walked, and mean little eyes and a big ring in his flared nostrils made him look like a bristly boar with a bad character.

"Who shall fight Dogsbreath?" repeated Gobber the Belch.

Ten of the boys stuck their hands up with cries of *"Oooosirmesirpleasechoosemesir,"* wildly excited at the thought of being smooshed into a pulp by Dogsbreath the Duhbrain. This was predictable. That's what most Hooligans were like.

But what was more surprising was that HICCUP also leapt to his feet, shouting, "I nominate myself, Hiccup Horrendous Haddock the Third!"

This was unusual because while Hiccup was the only son of Chief Stoick the Vast, he was not what you might call "naturally sporty." He was nearly as bad at Bashyball, Thugger and all the other violent Viking games as his best friend Fishlegs.

And Fishlegs had a squint, a limp, numerous allergies and no coordination whatsoever.

"What has got into you?" whispered Fishlegs. "Sit down, you lunatic. . . . He'll murder you. . . ."

"Don't worry, Fishlegs," said Hiccup, "I know what I'm doing here."

"Okay, HICCUP," boomed Gobber in surprise. "Get up here, boy, and show us what you're made of."

"If I'm EVER going to be Chief of this Tribe," whispered Hiccup to Fishlegs, as he started taking off his jacket and buckling on his sword, "I'm going to have to be a Hero at something. . . ."

"Trust me," said Fishlegs, "THIS IS NOT YOUR THING. . . . Clever ideas, yes. Talking to dragons, yes. But one-to-one combat with a brute like Dogsbreath? Absolutely NO, NO, NO."

Hiccup ignored him. "The Horrendous Haddocks have always had a gift for swordfighting. I reckon it's in the blood. . . . Look at my great-great-grandfather, Grimbeard the Ghastly. Best swordfighter EVER...."

"Yes, but have YOU ever done any swordfighting before?" asked Fishlegs.

"Well, no," admitted Hiccup, "but I've read books on it. I know all the moves.... The Piercing Lunge ... The Destroyer's Defense ... Grimbeard's Grapple ... And I've got this great new sword...."

The sword was, indeed, an excellent one, a Swiftpoint Scaremaker with go-faster stripes and a handle shaped like a hammerhead shark.

Swiftpoint Scaremaker

"Besides," said Hiccup, "I'm never going to be in actual danger...."

The Pirates-in-Training practiced with wooden cases on their swords. "Mollycoddling, we never did that in MY DAY," was Gobber's opinion. However, it DID mean the Hooligan Tribe ended up with more live Pirates at the end of the Program.

Fishlegs sighed. "Okay, you madman. If you have to do this ... keep looking in his eyes .... keep your sword up at all times ... and say a big prayer to Thor the Thunderer because you're going to need all the help you can get...."

2. THE FIGHT WITH DOGS-BREATH THE DUHBRAIN

Dogsbreath stood, pawing the deck in anticipation.

"KILL HIM, DOGSBREATH!" shouted Snotface Snotlout, Dogsbreath's friend and fellow bully.

Snotlout LOATHED Hiccup.

"I will," grinned Dogsbreath.

"This will be a massacre," hissed Dogsbreath's dragon Seaslug, an ugly great Gronckle with a pug nose and a mean temper. "My master will tear this Hiccup limb from limb and throw him to the gulls."

"D-d-don't bet on it," said Toothless, without a lot of conviction, and he gave Seaslug a sharp nip on the tail before scrambling for cover underneath one of the rowing benches.

Hiccup edged forward towards the hulking figure of Dogsbreath, swallowing hard. He tried to remember what *The Hero's Handbook* had said about swordfighting an opponent much bigger than yourself. . . . Something about ducking about, letting the enemy exhaust himself, using his own body weight against him. . . .

Dogsbreath the Duhbrain

"D-d-don't let him c-c-catch you!" advised Toothless, appearing for a moment from underneath the bench and then diving back into his hiding place as Seaslug lunged at him with a crunching crash of razor-sharp teeth.

Hiccup stepped forward lightly and calmly, looking Dogsbreath straight in the mean, piggy little eyes.

Dogsbreath grinned nastily at him, and aimed a huge flailing swipe at his head.

Hiccup ducked.

"Yay, HICCUP!" cheered Fishlegs. "That's the way to do it!"

Dogsbreath looked rather surprised. He swiped at Hiccup again, even more violently.

And again Hiccup ducked.

This time he was so quick about it that Dogsbreath staggered and nearly lost his footing.

"HIC-CUP! HIC-CUP! HIC-CUP!" yelled most of the boys. (Hiccup was popular with the other boys at the time because a month before he had single-handedly killed a Sea Dragon that threatened the whole Tribe.)*

---

* See *How to Train Your Dragon,* the first volume of Hiccup's memoirs.

I can Do this

Hiccup felt a little bubble of happiness somewhere inside him.

This was great.

Now Dogsbreath was getting cross. He snorted furiously, and lunged forward straight at Hiccup's heart. Hiccup dodged nimbly out of the way and . . . slipped on a slimy piece of the deck and . . . Dogsbreath reached out one meaty fist and . . . grabbed Hiccup by the back of the shirt and caught him.

This was not so great.

"Okay," thought Hiccup. "So he's caught me. What do I do now then?"

Toothless burst out from underneath the bench and hovered for a second or two, three inches from Hiccup's nose, shrieking, "S-S-SUBMIT! S-S-SUBMIT! S-S-SUBMIT!" at the top of his voice before zooming back to safety.

"I can't submit," said Hiccup indignantly.

"I'm supposed to be this Pirate Hero. Pirates don't submit."

"Oh goodee," said Dogsbreath happily before whacking Hiccup briskly on the helmet a few times with his sword. Hiccup tried to stop him, but each time he was too slow to protect himself.

"This is just embarrassing," thought Hiccup as Dogsbreath's sword clanged off his helmet for the third time. "Time to try a few moves."

He had a go at the Destroyer's Defense. He could see himself in his mind's eye, elegant, stylish. But when his brain tried to tell his arm what to do, his arm responded in this clumsy, fumbling way, and Dogsbreath grabbed hold of the fancy Swiftpoint Scaremaker and threw it over the side into the ocean.

There were hoots and jeers from the watching Vikings.

Fishlegs and Toothless winced. "Toothless can't l-l-look," moaned Toothless, with his wings over his eyes. "S-S-SUBMIT, you stupid human."

"What are you going to do, Hiccup?" sneered Snotlout. "Fight him with your bare hands? Or SUBMIT?"

"No way," said Hiccup stubbornly.

Dogsbreath moved in for the kill with a few breath-quenching jabs to the stomach. "Oh for THOR'S SAKE, Hiccup," yelled Gobber in exasperation. "You're fighting like an infant. You're not going to get anywhere by lying on the floor groaning. Bite him on the ankle or SOMETHING."

"He's USELESS," crowed Snotlout gleefully. "Hiccup the Useless, didn't I tell you? All that Dragon-Killing last month was just a fluke. USE-LESS, USE-LESS, USE-LESS. . . ."

Boys are very fickle. Hiccup's popularity vanished on the spot. They started chanting, "USE-LESS, USE-LESS, USE-LESS. . . ."

The dragons joined in eagerly.

"Scratch his eyes out!" screeched Brightclaw.

"Tear his wings off!" howled Fireworm.

"S-s-submit," moaned Toothless.

With a snort of satisfaction, Dogsbreath threw away his own sword and got down to the business he really enjoyed, hand-to-hand combat. Dogsbreath was an artist in his own sweet way. He liked to get the feel of his victim's flesh in his bare hands, like a sculptor with his clay.

Dogsbreath began by sitting on Hiccup, to the huge cheers of the rest of the boys. He followed this by scrunching Hiccup's face into the deck and twisting his ear at the same time.

"Oh suffering scallops," said Fishlegs, shutting his eyes. "I can't watch this. YOU CAN STILL DO IT, HICCUP!" he shouted. "USE HIS BODY WEIGHT AGAINST HIM!"

"And just how," inquired Hiccup out of one corner of his mashed mouth, "am I supposed to do that with him sitting on top of me?"

While everybody was concentrating on watching this massacre, Snotlout sneakily picked up Dogsbreath's sword and removed the wooden case.

"SUBMIT! SUBMIT! SUBMIT!" yelled Dogsbreath, gleefully bouncing up and down.

"No," said Hiccup.

"Maybe ickle Hiccup is going to start cwying," crowed Snotlout.

"USE-LESS, USE-LESS, USE-LESS," chanted the boys.

It was too tempting...

Toothless emerged from beneath Wartihog's bench. He looked left and right for any sign of Seaslug. And there, only inches away, was Dogsbreath's gigantic quivering bottom. It was too tempting. Toothless unlocked his jaws as wide as they would go.

As his name suggests, Toothless was entirely fang free. But his hard little gums could slice through the shell of an oyster and crush the claws of a crab. . . .

He leapt forward and BIT that wobbling rear end as hard as he could.

"OOOOOOOW!" howled Dogsbreath, letting go of Hiccup, who scrambled out of his way as quickly as he could.

Now Dogsbreath was really, *really* mad.

He grabbed hold of his sword, not realizing or caring that it no longer had a wooden case on it, and lunged wildly at Hiccup. Hiccup leapt out of the way, but the sharp point of the blade pierced his shirt and tore a neat slice out of it.

"Uh-oh," said Hiccup, suddenly realizing he was in Big Trouble. "Dogsbreath, your sword has lost its . . ."

But Dogsbreath wasn't listening. He gave a roar of maddened fury, and made a great slashing swipe at Hiccup's head. Hiccup ducked and the wickedly sharp blade buried itself in the mast of the boat, slicing the top off one of the horns on Hiccup's helmet in the process.

"STOP!" cried Hiccup from behind the mast, as Dogsbreath tugged furiously at his sword to pull it free. "Your sword has lost its case, you're going to KILL ME...."

But Dogsbreath was so angry he could not hear a thing. He gave a great heave with his mighty muscles and the sword jerked free so suddenly that the poor brute sat down heavily on his bottom, just on that tender spot where Toothless had taken a big chunk out of it.

"YOOOOOOOOW!" yelled Dogsbreath.

"HA HA HA HA HA!" laughed the boys.

Dogsbreath staggered to his feet, as mad as a harpooned whale. He threw himself at Hiccup with great bellows of fury. Although Hiccup managed to avoid him again, this time he slipped over in the process. Dogsbreath pinned him down with

one giant hand, and he lifted his sword above his head
with the other.

"DON'T DO IT!" shouted Hiccup desperately,
but Dogsbreath's eyes were full of the joys of battle
and he began to swing the blade down towards
Hiccup's chest.

And that would have been the end of Hiccup
if it hadn't been for the extraordinarily lucky

coincidence that at that very moment the ship lurched
queasily upwards on the next giant wave, rolled for
a second on the brim, and plunged hysterically
downwards . . . straight onto a large floating object
that instantly holed the boat.

"Abandon ship!" shrieked Fireworm, and thirteen
dragons rose into the air like gigantic bats. (Dragons are
only loyal to their Masters up to a certain point.)

The ship split into two pieces on the spot,
spilling the Vikings out into the sea. It then sank,
with a sigh of relief, to the bottom of the ocean bed
in about ten seconds flat.

One minute Hiccup was in the not-so-loving
embrace of Dogsbreath the Duhbrain, the next
he was doing the doggy paddle in water so breath-
quenchingly, spine-numbingly, heart-stoppingly cold that
it was difficult to think of questions like: "What in
Woden's name do we do now?"

Something landed with a bump on the top
of Hiccup's helmet. Toothless's eyes peered into his,
upside down.

"N-n-nice fighting, Master," he said.
"N-n-now, where's my l-l-lunch?"

"You may not have noticed," said Hiccup,

swallowing a big chunk of seawater as the weight of Toothless pushed him under the surface, "but I'm having a bit of a crisis here. Now flap off, will you, and see what's happened to Fishlegs. He can't swim."

Hiccup *could* swim but the waves were mountainously rough. He really had to struggle to keep afloat.

Toothless returned a moment or so later looking anxious.

"F-f-fishlegs d-d-definitely needs your help, Master. B-b-big trouble. Follow me."

And he disappeared again.

Hiccup was just thinking, "Well, I don't know what in Valhalla he thinks I can do about it," when a miracle occurred.

3. A CHANCE IN A MILLION

The object that had holed the boat, thereby saving
Hiccup from Death at the hands of Dogsbreath
the Duhbrain, was a large, heavy, six-foot-by-three-
foot BOX.

It now floated up to within reaching distance
of where Hiccup was treading water. There were a
couple of iron handles on the sides, very handy for
grabbing on to.

About twenty minutes earlier, some laughing
members of the Meathead Tribe had thrown this box
into the sea at Meathead Island, which was a couple of
miles away. The winds had carried it a considerable
distance in that short time.

And the chances of that particular box traveling
all that way, and then in the middle of the whole wild
and lonely ocean happening to hole the ship just in
time to save Hiccup's life, must have been thousands,
no, millions to one.

If you were a fanciful person, you might have
said that it was almost as if that box was *looking*
for Hiccup.

But we are not fanciful people, and that would be ridiculous.

No sooner had Hiccup grabbed hold of one of the iron handles with a sigh of relief than a gigantic wave lifted him and the box way, way up, and then deposited them crashing down only a couple of feet away from where Toothless was trying to keep Fishlegs from going under for the third and what would have been final time.

The dragon had a firm grip on the back of Fishlegs's shirt, his wings were flapping furiously, and his little green face had turned bright red with the effort of trying to stop Fishlegs from sinking.

Fishlegs had got hold of a piece of broken oar that was keeping him up a bit, but he couldn't cling on much longer, and he would have drowned if it had not been for the sudden arrival of Hiccup and the mysterious box.

There was a lull in the sea for a couple of moments, in which Hiccup and Toothless managed to heave the exhausted Fishlegs onto the top of the box.

And there he clung, like an anxious Daddy Long-legs, terrified but alive.

Five indescribably cold minutes later, they were

blown by the violence of the wind onto the shores of the Long Beach. Amazingly, all thirteen of the boys and Gobber himself had survived the shipwreck.

Gobber didn't exactly give them a big, welcoming hug.

"Mmmm, good work I suppose," he said begrudgingly, sniffing a bit. "You took your time about it, though. Step lively, Fishlegs. We're horribly late for the next lesson."

As soon as Fishlegs had dragged himself off the box and collapsed panting onto the beach, Gobber stopped being irritated.

Because the box wasn't a box at all.

It was a coffin.

A huge, six-and-a-half-foot floating coffin, with the following words carved into the lid:

BEWARE!
DO NOT OPEN THIS COFFIN

4. WHOSE COFFIN IS THIS ANYWAY?

The boys all crowded around the box, forgetting, in their curiosity, about their narrow escape from drowning.

"It's a coffin, sir."

"Yes, I can see that, thank you, Wartihog," snapped Gobber the Belch. "The question is, whose?"

The answer was written right underneath the words "Do Not Open This Coffin," in letters scratched out with some kind of dagger, and stained with something that might once have been blood.

"CURSED BE HE WHO DISTURBS THE REMAINS OF GRIMBEARD THE GHASTLY, THE GREATEST PIRATE WHO EVER STRUCK TERROR INTO THE INNER ISLES."

Hiccup felt a cold clammy shiver run down his back, and he suddenly knew that something really bad was going to happen.

Grimbeard the Ghastly had been Hiccup's own great-great-grandfather.

"The Lost Treasure of Grimbeard the Ghastly" was a popular Hooligan Saga. It told of how

Grimbeard had won a glorious treasure through his brilliance at piracy and swordfighting, a treasure that included his famous sword, the Stormblade.

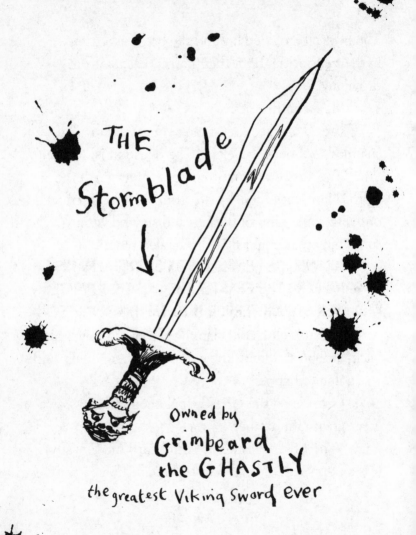

THE
Stormblade
↓

Owned by
Grimbeard
the GHASTLY
the greatest Viking sword ever

But after twenty years of glorious rule, Grimbeard
had disappeared on a mysterious quest, and neither
he nor the treasure were ever seen again.

And now here, out of the blue, one hundred years
later, his coffin had appeared back on the shores of
Berk. . . . It was spooky.

"OOOOOOOOH," chattered Wartihog in
excitement. "Do you think there might be
TREASURE in there, sir? Can we open it, sir?
Pleasesir, pleasesir, can we open it?"

All the other boys joined in the clamor . . .
except for Hiccup.

Hiccup knew that Grimbeard had been the
ULTIMATE in pirate-ness, the GREEDIEST,
GRISLIEST, GORIEST Viking who had ever sailed
and slew and farted his way across the Northern Seas.

Treasure or no treasure, if a man like Grimbeard
the Ghastly was telling you not to mess with his
coffin, it was Hiccup's personal opinion that you ought
to listen.

Even if he had been dead for a hundred years.

Particularly if he had been dead for a
hundred years.

"Right," said Gobber, just as excited as

everybody else, "we're going to have to forget about the Advanced Rudery lesson. This is an Important Discovery and I think we should take it straight to Stoick the Vast and the Council of Elders. Bearhug, Sharpknife, Wartihog, Clueless, pick it up and carry it back to the Hooligan Village. . . ."

The boys hauled the coffin onto their shoulders.

"Don't just hang about shivering, you lazy lug-fish," Gobber bellowed crazily. "This is Pirate Training, not a holiday with your mother on the Mainland. QUICK MARCH, one-two, one-two, one-two. . . ."

He set off at a brisk trot towards the Hooligan Village.

The boys sighed and began to stumble after him.

Snotlout and Dogsbreath the Duhbrain sauntered over to Hiccup, who was sitting, trying to catch his breath on a large rock, shivering violently.

"A shame that Dogsbreath was interrupted," sneered Snotlout, "just when things were getting interesting, don't you think, Dogsbreath?"

"Yeah," grinned Dogsbreath the Duhbrain.

"I reckon," said Snotlout thoughtfully to the remaining boys, "that Hiccup must be the most pathetic swordfighter I have EVER seen, don't you think, guys? I mean, face it, Hiccup, somebody who fights like a granny with a back problem is NEVER going to be Chief of this Tribe. . . ."

"Oh, and so who *is* going to be Chief of this Tribe if Hiccup isn't?" asked Fishlegs, still lying spread-eagled on the sand in the exact position where he had fallen off the coffin. "Let me guess . . . YOU, I suppose?"

Snotlout flexed his muscles, making the skeleton tattooed on his right biceps grin smugly.

"I AM the obvious choice," he said. "I've got noble blood" (Snotlout was Hiccup's cousin, the son of Baggybum the Beerbelly, the Chief's younger brother), "charisma, good looks" (Snotlout stroked the rather unpleasant little straggly hairs on his upper lip that he was trying to grow into a mustache), "and I'm BRILLIANT at absolutely everything. . . ."

Unfortunately this was true.

Snotlout was a natural at Mindless Violence, superb at Advanced Rudery and practically everything else.

". . . particularly swordfighting," said Snotlout, drawing his sword from its scabbard.

The other boys gasped.

"Wow," breathed Speedifist. "The latest Double-Sided Extra-Biting Supa-Sword. Curving inner edges, silverpoint finish . . . where did you get THAT from, Snotlout?"

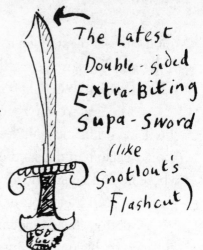

The Latest Double-Sided Extra-Biting Supa-Sword (like Snotlout's Flashcut)

"This is the Flashcut," boasted Snotlout, swishing the beautiful sword around so that everybody could get a good look. "Makes that silly Swiftpoint Scaremaker that Dogsbreath lost for you look pretty weak, doesn't it, Hiccup? Let me show you how swordfighting should be done. This," sneered Snotlout, lunging athletically, "is a Perfect Pointer. . . ."

Hiccup dodged.

"And this is the Destroyer's Defense. . . ." Snotlout gave an animal howl and brought the sword down over his head, stopping just before he cut Hiccup in half.

"And that," jeered Snotlout, slashing the Flashcut expertly from side to side and then leaping forward suddenly, the sword ending up just inches away from

Hiccup's heart, "*that* is a Grimbeard's Grapple. . . .
But I expect a loser like you, who couldn't even
beat a three-year-old in diapers, hasn't even *heard*
of moves like that."

Hiccup said nothing.

"THAT, dear cousin," sneered Snotlout,
"is HOW TO SWORDFIGHT." He put his sword
back in its scabbard.

"Yup," he said, very pleased with himself,
"I'm a genius. I'm going to make the best Chief this
Tribe has ever had."

"It's just a shame," said Fishlegs, "that your brain
isn't as big as one of your nostrils."

Snotlout looked irritated for a second as all the
other boys laughed. He grabbed Hiccup by the scruff
of the neck and lifted him clear off the ground.

"Amazing how the wooden case to that sword
fell off, wasn't it?" he spat right into Hiccup's face.
"You were lucky this time . . . but the question is, can
you be lucky ALL the time? Think about it, LOSER.
Come on, Dogsbreath. Let's leave the girlies to get
their beauty sleep."

He dropped Hiccup and as he went he trod
heavily and deliberately on one of Fishlegs's hands.

"Whoops," laughed Snotlout.

"Har Har Har Har," snorted Dogsbreath the Duhbrain.

And they jogged off.

"If Snotlout is EVER Chief of this Tribe, I'm emigrating," said Fishlegs, shaking his hand.

"Are you all right, Fishlegs?" asked Hiccup with concern, as he gazed down on Fishlegs still lying flat on his back.

"Perfect," croaked Fishlegs, coughing up a bit more seawater. "I do love an early morning swim. How about you?"

"Oh, couldn't be better really," said Hiccup bleakly, taking off one of his boots and pouring out a flood of seawater and a couple of small fish.

"My first day at Pirate Training and I've already been humiliated by my pathetic swordfighting, beaten to a pulp, shipwrecked, and narrowly escaped Death by drowning. And it's not even ten o'clock yet."

"Maybe it was the SWORD that was the problem," suggested Fishlegs kindly but untruthfully.

Hiccup brightened up.

"You could be right," he said eagerly. "It felt a bit light in my hands. Perhaps I need something a bit chunkier, you know, to get some weight behind my swing." He did a few imaginary lunges in the air. "That must be it, because I still have this feeling that swordfighting is going to be my thing, you know?"

"Um, yeeeessss," said Fishlegs, not wanting to hurt Hiccup's feelings by mentioning that it had been the worst display of swordfighting he had seen, EVER. "And you need a lot more PRACTICE, don't you think?"

Hiccup nodded enthusiastically. "Anyway," he said, "we need to get after the others. I'm freezing, and I've a horrible feeling that some idiot is going to suggest OPENING that coffin which says quite clearly DO NOT OPEN. It would be just the sort of mindlessly stupid thing they would do."

"What do you think could be in it?" asked Fishlegs.

"I don't know," said Hiccup, "but a pirate like Grimbeard the Ghastly won't have hidden the treasure in it without booby-trapping it in some way. You read what it said on the top. . . . A man like him could have thought of all SORTS of unpleasant surprises."

Fishlegs sighed and struggled to his feet. They set off slowly towards the Hooligan Village, Toothless hitching a ride on Hiccup's helmet.

"They wouldn't open it, would they?" worried Fishlegs. "Surely, surely, SURELY, they couldn't be that stupid?"

Grimbeard the GHASTLY

5. DO NOT OPEN a Coffin That Says "DO NOT OPEN" on the Front

As soon as they got to the Hooligan Village, Hiccup and Fishlegs changed into dry(ish) clothes. (Berk was one of those damp places where clothes never really dried. They just became warm and wet rather than cold and wet.)

They hurried as quickly as they could towards the Great Hall.

By the time they got there, Stoick had called a Big Meeting of Everybody and the Great Hall was already packed to bursting with great Hairy Hooligans jostling each other for a good view of the coffin, which had been placed on a table in front of the fire.

Bit by bit Hiccup and Fishlegs managed to wriggle their way through the crowd to the front.

"Ah, Hiccup, there you are," said Hiccup's father Stoick the Vast absentmindedly, as he consulted with the other Elders in front of the coffin.

Stoick was a terrifying red-headed bull of a man whose belly turned a corner a good foot or two before the rest of him.

"Interesting find you've made here, my boy," said Stoick, ruffling his son's hair proudly. "The Lost Treasure of Grimbeard the Ghastly, eh?"

"Yes, Father, but . . . ," said Hiccup.

"We're just about to open it," said Stoick.

"But what *I'm* trying to say is," interrupted Old Wrinkly (the cleverest and most ancient Elder of the Hooligan Tribe), "it is written quite clearly on the top, 'DO NOT OPEN THIS COFFIN, Cursed be he who disturbs the remains of Grimbeard the Ghastly, the greatest pirate who ever struck Terror into the Inner Isles.' . . . In my considerable experience it is always a good idea NOT TO OPEN a coffin that says 'DO NOT OPEN' on the front. . . ."

"I agree," said Hiccup nervously. "Grimbeard

Stoick the Vast
thinking

<u>NOW,</u> what would a GREAT
LEADER do in this situation?

the Ghastly was a nasty piece of work. Anybody who opens that coffin could be in for a horrible shock."

"Rubbish," scoffed Stoick the Vast. "A warning like that to put off grave robbers should not stay the hand of Fearsome Vikings like ourselves. Shall we, who laugh in the face of Death and spit in the eye of the Great Typhoon, quail at a simple curse to scare infants and old men?"

Cries of "No!" and "Not likely, guv'nor!"

"All those in favor of opening up the box and seeing whether the Lost Treasure of Grimbeard the Ghastly is inside say AYE!"

"AYE!!!" bellowed out every member of the Hooligan Tribe, except for Fishlegs, Old Wrinkly and Hiccup.

"R-r-run for your lives!" yelped Toothless, and hid in Hiccup's shirt. Fishlegs edged backwards into the crowd.

"NOT a good idea, NOT a good idea, NOT a good idea," muttered Hiccup. He started backing away from the coffin as Stoick fiddled clumsily with the iron clasps.

"NOT a good idea, NOT a good idea, NOT A GOOD IDEA," repeated Hiccup as Stoick slowly c-r-e-a-k-e-d up the coffin lid. . . .

c-r-e-e-e-e-e-e-e-e-e-e-e-e-e-e-a-k. . .

The coffin lid dropped open with a bang.

Stoick jumped away to avoid being splashed by the seawater gushing out of it from all sides.

Everybody else tried very hard not to look nervous. Stoick peered into the coffin.

There was a bit of a pause.

"Not pretty, was he?" sniffed Stoick the Vast, trying to show off how much he laughed in the face of Death.

"Oh, I don't know, sir," said Gobber the Belch, leaning in to look as well. "I think I can see a bit of a family resemblance."

"I know what you mean," said Baggybum the Beerbelly, turning his head thoughtfully. "There's a look of Great-Aunt Heftythighs."

Hiccup forced himself to open his eyes. If he was ever going to be a pirate, he would have to get used to this sort of thing. He made himself peer over the edge and into the coffin.

There, in a state of green and yellow decay, lay the corpse of Grimbeard the Ghastly. It wasn't so bad really. The face was all slimy and drippy, but it wasn't crawling with maggots or anything disgusting. Rather peaceful really, lying so still. . . .

And then Hiccup was sure he saw one of the paper-white fingers twitch slightly.

He blinked and stared hard at it.

Nothing for a second.

And then . . . there it was again, a definite quivering. . . .

"The c-c-corpse!" stuttered Hiccup. "It's m-m-moving!"

"Nonsense, boy!" snapped Gobber the Belch. "How can he possibly move? He's DEAD, isn't he?" And he gave the corpse a prod with one fat forefinger.

The corpse of Grimbeard the Ghastly snapped straight upright, propelled by some appalling force from within it, yellow eyes popping, dribbly green face contorted in a ghastly grimace.

"Aaaaaargh," gurgled the corpse of Grimbeard the Ghastly, straight into the face of Gobber the Belch.

"AAAAAAAAAAAAAAAAAAARGH!"
screeched Gobber the Belch, jumping quite three feet
in the air with his hair and his beard sticking out in all
directions with the shock of it.

"AAAAAAAAAAAAAAAAAAARGH!" yelled
the rest of the Tribe.

For while Hooligans do indeed laugh in the face
of Death and spit in the eye of the Great Typhoon,
they have a morbid fear of the SUPERNATURAL.

Stoick dived underneath the table with his arms
over his head in the vague belief that if he couldn't
see IT, IT couldn't see HIM.

Seawater poured out of the coffin. The corpse
of Grimbeard the Ghastly made disgusting choking
noises. The veins on its popping yellow eyes stood out,
its grey mouth quivered horribly.

Only Old Wrinkly remained calm.

"Don't panic," said Old Wrinkly, "this is
NOT the corpse of Grimbeard the Ghastly. . . ."

Hiccup had frozen in sheer terror. But he
trusted Old Wrinkly, and he opened his eyes.

Nobody else took any notice whatsoever.
They went on panicking like crazy.

Gobber
the Belch
jumped quite
three feet
in the air
with the
shock of
it...

"Woden preserve me from the terminally stupid,"
muttered Old Wrinkly under his breath, and he
started yelling, as this was the only language the
Hooligans really understood. "DON'T PANIC! THIS
IS NOT THE CORPSE OF GRIMBEARD THE
GHASTLY!"

As he yelled he patted the corpse-that-wasn't-a-
corpse hard on the back. Seawater spluttered out of
it in all directions, gushing out of its nose and ears
and mouth.

It wasn't the corpse of Grimbeard the Ghastly.
Now that it had recovered from its coughing fit,
it was clearly a tall, good-looking man, very much alive,
if a little green from the effects of the seawater.

"So . . . ," said Stoick, from under the table, "that
is DEFINITELY NOT the corpse of Grimbeard the
Ghastly?"

The corpse-that-wasn't-a-corpse shook its head.

"Oh no," it said faintly, "definitely not. Easy
mistake to make, but no, I'm not."

And it slithered out of the coffin in a rush
of seawater. It removed its helmet and, under the
circumstances, performed a remarkably
graceful bow.

46

"The name is Alvin. Alvin the . . . er . . . Poor-but-Honest Farmer."

Alvin had quick, clever, laughing eyes. He had a long, elegant mustache, a little limp from the seawater. He smiled a charming, easygoing smile (although a fussy person might think that perhaps it had too many teeth in it).

Alvin stepped gracefully forward to pat Hiccup on the head.

"And who might YOU be then, sonny?"

"H-Hiccup Horrendous Haddock the Third," stammered Hiccup.

"Greetings," said Alvin the Poor-but-Honest Farmer.

He stooped to peer under the table. "I presume from your air of natural authority that you must be the Chief of this Tribe?"

"Stoick the Vast," replied Stoick.

Alvin clapped a hand to his forehead.

"Not THE Stoick the Vast, Terror of the Seas, Most High Ruler of the Hairy Hooligans, O Hear His Name and Tremble, Ugh, Ugh? By an EXTRAORDINARY coincidence, you are the very man I have been searching for."

47

Stoick crawled out from under the table, staggered to his feet and puffed out his chest.

"That's me," said Stoick the Vast, in much of his old hearty manner. "And, may I ask, if you're *not* the corpse of Grimbeard the Ghastly, what in Woden's name were you doing in his coffin?"

"What a remarkably bright question," replied Alvin enthusiastically, "and if I could just sit down in this comfortable-looking chair? It's been a long day. . . ."

"Of course, of course," said Stoick, dusting off his throne.

". . . I would be delighted to tell you my Tale . . . ," said Alvin.

Toothless didn't like the look of Alvin...

6. THE TALE OF ALVIN THE POOR-BUT-HONEST FARMER

The whole of the Tribe of Hairy Hooligans sat round-eyed, in silence, as Alvin settled himself into Stoick's throne and told his Tale.

"I was put in the coffin," began Alvin, "by some very rude people who not only disbelieved the Tale I am about to tell you but also suspected me of being a common thief. They dumped me over the side of the Harbor on their island with a lot of rude laughter. . . ."

"Meatheads," said Stoick knowledgeably. "Were they led by a tall chap, one eye, bad breath, answers to the name of Mogadon?"

"That does ring a bell," admitted Alvin.

"But how had you come across the coffin in the first place?" asked Stoick.

"I am a poor-but-honest farmer," said Alvin, "and a long time ago in the Peaceable Country, far far away, I was digging up some ground for . . . er . . . planting potatoes when I came across this coffin which . . . er . . . just fell open in my hands."

"And when you opened this coffin which says

49

Alvin the
Poor-But-Honest-Farmer

quite clearly 'DO NOT OPEN' on the front," asked Old Wrinkly thoughtfully, "was there not some sort of surprise?"

"You could say that," admitted Alvin with a good-natured smile that perhaps did not quite reach his eyes. "I opened the coffin, reached forward quite innocently to grasp something inside . . . and the coffin lid snapped shut with the force of a shark's jaws and in one stroke cut off my hand."

Alvin held up his right arm.

There, where his hand should have been emerging from his sleeve, was an iron claw.

The Hooligans gasped in horror.

"Dearie me," tutted Stoick. "BOOBY-TRAPPED. I do apologize for my great-grandfather. He did have a nasty sense of humor."

"Yeeesss," said Alvin, smiling happily once more, "but luckily us Poor-but-Honest Farmers can take a joke. . . . And this," he gestured to the claw, "is very handy for opening up oysters. . . . Now, back to my Tale. I was careful the next time I opened the coffin to dismantle the booby trap first, but there was no sign of any Treasure inside, nor indeed the body of Grimbeard the Ghastly. . . . What there *was* . . ."

The entire Tribe of Hairy Hooligans leaned forward eagerly, mouths open, eyes wide. . . .

". . . was *this* map*, and *this* riddle."

Alvin reached into his breast pocket and held up the map and the riddle for everybody to see.

"Oh," said Stoick, very disappointed. "No Grimbeard? No treasure? No Stormblade? Just two little pieces of paper?"

"Ah, but Stoick," said Alvin craftily, "these two little pieces of paper will LEAD us to Grimbeard's treasure."

"US?" said Old Wrinkly. "Something is puzzling me. You have the riddle, you have the map, why didn't you just go and find the treasure yourself? Why did you come here to us?"

"But that would be dishonest!" said Alvin virtuously. "We all know the Saga of 'The Lost Treasure of Grimbeard the Ghastly.' . . . This treasure belongs to you, his descendants. Besides, there's the little matter of the riddle. The riddle makes it clear that this treasure cannot be found by just *anybody*."

Alvin cleared his throat.

---

* See page viii for the Treasure Map of Grimbeard the Ghastly.

Dare you brave the watery grave?
The Death's Head prick of fire and sleep?
If you dare you are my Heir
For my Heir's Beast shall sniff it there
And he shall tell me underground
Am I lost or am I found?

"So you see," said Alvin, "it seems only the Heir to Grimbeard the Ghastly can find the treasure. . . . And only his beast can sniff it out. I assume by 'Beast' he means dragon."

Dragons were excellent sniffers and finders of Treasure. A good dragon could sniff out gold and precious metals even when they were buried some way below ground.

"And I couldn't possibly find this treasure myself," said Alvin, "because I don't have a way with dragons. They just DON'T LIKE ME, I don't know what it is. Anyway, I wonder if any of you have any idea of where the riddle is talking about? You, for instance,

Stoick, with your quick and lively brain?"

Stoick struggled to look intelligent. "Hmmmm, it's a hard one. . . ."

Hiccup looked at the map.

"Don't you think the Death's Head might be talking about the Isle of the Skullions, Father?" suggested Hiccup. "A Death's Head is a skull, after all. . . ."

"Of course!" boomed Stoick. "The Isle of the Skullions! That'll be where it is!"

The Isle of the Skullions was a small island off the west coast of Berk that formed the shape of a skull and crossbones. It was this shape that Grimbeard had adopted for his flag and, most famously, his helmet.

"So this island here is the Isle of the Skullions, is it?" purred Alvin gleefully, pointing at the map. "And that's where we'll find our treasure?"

To Alvin's surprise the Hooligans started laughing.

"Oh, there's no question of finding the treasure if it's on the Isle of the Skullions," said Stoick cheerfully. "Nobody has *ever* returned from the Isle of the Skullions ALIVE. Hiccup, you're the expert on dragons, you explain to Alvin about Skullions. . . ."

The SKULLION

The Skullion is a dragon standing about ten feet tall. It has lost the power of flight, eyesight and hearing but its sense of smell is phenomenal and it will eat anything it comes across. This animal is untrainable and very, very dangerous.

~ STATISTICS ~

COLORS: Black and purple.

ARMED WITH: Terrifying teeth, claws etc...... 9

RADAR: Yes, also strong sense of smell 7

POISON: None 0

HUNTING ABILITY:
You don't want to be the prey 9

SPEED: Very, very fast 9

FEAR AND FIGHT FACTOR:
Nasty — unprecedented savagery*...... 8 or 9.

* (but you do have a chance because they can't see or hear)

"The Skullion," said Hiccup, always delighted to be asked a natural-history question, "is a very rare, very savage species of flightless dragon. Despite being blind and very nearly deaf, it is one of the most fearsome predators of all dragons, hunting in packs using a highly developed sense of smell alone. . . ."

"Okay, okay," said Stoick hurriedly, "we get the picture. . . ."

"It has this one extra-long super-sharp claw," continued Hiccup, "with which it disables its victims by cutting the Achilles tendon at the back of their heels, leaving them unable to walk. It then eats them alive."

NOT very nice.

"Ahhhhh," said Alvin. "I see the problem. But I am sure a man as clever as you, Stoick, will be able to lead a quest to the Isle of the Skullions to find this treasure nonetheless."

"A quest to the Isle of the Skullions would be total madness," said Old Wrinkly firmly.

"Grimbeard's sword, the Stormblade, will be part of this treasure," wheedled Alvin. "And if you held the Stormblade the name of Hooligan would be feared again throughout the barbarian world. . . ."

Stoick stroked his beard thoughtfully.

"And you, Stoick," cooed Alvin, "picture yourself with diamonds sprinkled in your beard, a golden breastplate, the Stormblade flaming terribly in one hand, bracelets for those handsome wrists of yours. I can see you already, Mogadon kneeling humbly before you. What a vision you will be!"

Stoick sucked in his belly and flexed his muscles. He'd always secretly fancied himself in a pair of earrings.

"I'LL DO IT!" he yelled.

"FELLOW HOOLIGANS!" he bellowed. "I shall lead you on a quest to find the treasure of our ancestors!"

"But it's insane!" cried Hiccup. "Anyone who sets one toe on that island will be eaten alive in moments! It's suicide to even think of it!"

Everyone was cheering too hard to listen to Hiccup.

"Glory and riches shall be ours," beamed Stoick, patting Alvin painfully hard on the back.

"Oh, here we gooo . . . ," moaned Hiccup to himself.

7. PRACTICING SWORD-FIGHTING AND SNIFFING FOR TREASURE

In Hiccup's opinion, everything went wrong from the moment Alvin the Poor-but-Honest Farmer was let out of the coffin. It wasn't Alvin's fault, of course. He was a most entertaining and enjoyable companion.

He made the women blush by praising their muscles and their fat yellow plaits. He made the men laugh with hilarious farty jokes and impressions of Mogadon the Meathead. He made the children adore him by telling stories of the trickeries and battles of long-dead Heroes.

Hiccup liked him, too.

Alvin came across Hiccup one day, practicing his swordfighting for the second depressing hour in a row.

Hiccup was trying to do Grimbeard's Grapple, and failing miserably every time. Stoick had given him a new sword to replace the Scaremaker, an impressively large and heavy one called a Stretchapoint.

"Got a lot of LENGTH to it, my boy," Stoick had

said. "It'll make up for your shortness of arm. Give you a better reach."

But Hiccup had difficulty keeping it steady, and when he got to the lunge at the end he tended to fall over. He had just got up and wearily picked up the Stretchapoint for another go, when Alvin the Poor-but-Honest Farmer suddenly appeared right behind him and said, "Hiccup, isn't it?"

Hiccup was so startled he nearly fell over again. He hadn't realized he was being watched.

"You're the Heir to Stoick the Vast, aren't you?" smiled Alvin.

Hiccup sighed. "Well, I hope so," he said. "That's the general idea, anyway. But unless I get better at this swordfighting, I'm never going to be anybody's Heir. I'm HOPELESS at it."

The Stretchapoint
(for the short of arm)

extra sharp sides

"No, no," said Alvin reassuringly, "you've got natural ability, I can see that. You just need a little coaching, that's all. Let me show you."

Alvin carefully put his helmet by the side of the ferns for safekeeping. Hiccup watched, fascinated, as he untwisted the claw attached to his right arm. In its place he fixed a "sword-holder" mechanism. He then drew his sword and showed Hiccup how he could fit it into the mechanism. He twisted it tight so it wouldn't fall off.

"A clever little contraption I designed myself," said Alvin. "I think I even fight better now than I did before the accident. . . ." He twirled his mustache and demonstrated the Grapple himself.

"You see," said Alvin, "the weight should be kept on the left foot."

Hiccup followed him carefully . . . and fell over again.

"BRAVO!" clapped Alvin, to Hiccup's surprise.

"But I fell over again," said Hiccup.

"But with such STYLE," said Alvin. "You can't teach that, it's in the blood."

Alvin replaced the sword with the claw and picked up his helmet. He made a grimace as he put it back on his head. He took it off again and peered inside. "There seems to be some sort of MUD in here, some sort of very SMELLY mud. . . ."

"It's all over your hair, I'm afraid, sir," said Hiccup.

Alvin looked horrified. He was very particular about his personal appearance. He hurried away to wash it off.

Toothless, who had been hunting rats through

the ferns, came and perched on Hiccup's shoulder. He had the giggles.

Eventually, when he got his breath back, he choked out, "P-p-pooed in his helmet. . . ."

"TOOTHLESS!" scolded Hiccup. "That's revolting and unkind. Why did you poo in poor Alvin's helmet?"

"H-h-he's a BAD MAN," replied Toothless.

"Who, Alvin the Poor-but-Honest Farmer?" asked Hiccup in surprise. "Don't be so prejudiced, Toothless. Just because he's not from round these parts doesn't make him a bad man. . . ."

"S-s-suit yourself," shrugged Toothless, checking out his wings for dragonfleas. "Toothless thinks he's an O-O-Outcast."

Hiccup started nervously.

Outcasts were Vikings who were so vicious, so terrible and sneaking and burglarous, that they had been cast out of regular Viking society, and had formed an extraordinarily ferocious Tribe of their own. It was even rumored that some Outcasts ate their enemies.

"Oh, come ON," protested Hiccup. "He doesn't look anything LIKE an Outcast."

Toothless doing a poo in Alvin's helmet

"Y-y-you ever seen one?" asked Toothless.

"Well, no," admitted Hiccup, "but neither have you, and you haven't a shred of evidence. Let's go and get some lunch and forget this rubbish."

That conversation sowed a little seed of doubt in Hiccup's mind.

He was already feeling uneasy because he knew that he and all the other boys were going to have to join in this suicidal quest to the Isle of the Skullions, which would set out just as soon as Stoick and Alvin had worked out a Plan to avoid the Tiny Problem of everybody being eaten alive the moment they landed on the island.

And he knew that he, Hiccup, as the Heir to the Hairy Hooligans, was supposed to be the one to find the treasure. So when he wasn't doing his swordfighting, or being shouted at by Gobber on the Training Program, he was bustling Toothless out of the door to practice sniffing for treasure.

The first morning was typical. Fishlegs turned up with his dragon Horrorcow, and they stood watching in polite astonishment as Hiccup went through the elaborate game of getting Toothless out of the front door.

Firstly, Hiccup went through the house shouting Toothless's name.

No answer.

Next, Hiccup stole a mackerel from the pantry.

"Ohhhhh, Toothless," he sang craftily, waving the fishy stench around a bit to get Toothless's interest. "I've got a lovely piece of mackerel for you."

A very muffled but thoughtful voice replied, "T-t-toothless sick. T-t-toothless can't come out 'cos he's V-V-VERY VERY sick."

"Then you won't want this mackerel then," sang Hiccup.

Another pause.

"M-m-mackerel good for the sick. Have mackerel but NO GO OUT."

Hiccup had worked out where the voice was coming from. He peered up the chimney, and there was Toothless, hanging upside down in a cloud of smoke.

"NO, Toothless," said Hiccup in his firmest voice. "You have the mackerel, you have to go out, THAT'S the deal. And you have to PROMISE."

"Okay, then," said Toothless, flapping out of the chimney, "Toothless p-p-promise."

Hiccup held out the mackerel.

With a shriek of "T-T-TOOTHLESS CROSSED HIS CLAWS!" Toothless grabbed the fish, pushed Hiccup heavily in the chest, and disappeared at high speed into the other room, leaving Hiccup to topple over into the fireplace in a cloud of ash.

It didn't take long for Hiccup to find him again.

A telltale drift of bluey-gray smoke was curling out from the end of Stoick's bed.

Hiccup tiptoed up and dragged him out from under the covers.

With a squawk of outrage, Toothless grabbed hold of one of the bed knobs in his powerful jaws.

Hiccup got him by the tail and pulled.

"Come ON, Toothless," said Hiccup, "time for

LEARNING TO SPEAK DRAGONESE

Dragonese is punctuated by shrill shrieks
and popping noises, and sounds
MOST EXTRAORDINARY
when spoken by a human. The word
"pishyou," for example, is pronounced
very like a sneeze.

MORE COMMON DRAGON PHRASES:

Pishyou na munch-munch di miaow-miaow
Please do not eat the cat

≈

Hoody chuck-it-up un di jim-jams di pappa?
Who has been sick in my father's pajamas?

≈

**PARKA DI BOTTY, forsakes di Woden,
or me do di girly boo-hoo.**
SIT, for Woden's sake, before I burst into tears

(To big dragons): **Mi wobblediguts bigtime.**
I am very poisonous

sniffing practice. . . ." He tickled Toothless under one wing. Toothless wriggled a bit, going red in the face. Hiccup tickled him under the other.

Toothless let go, giggling, and there was a short kerfuffle, in which Toothless bit Hiccup several times, before Hiccup finally got him under control, tucking him under one arm and holding his mouth shut with the other.

"Now," said Hiccup, "you know we have to practice the sniffing. You want *us* to find the treasure, don't you, not Fireworm or Seaslug? You want us to show everybody what amazing sniffers Toothless Daydreams really are, don't you?"

Toothless nodded, still with Hiccup holding his mouth shut.

"Well, then," said Hiccup, "we have to practice. Promise you won't bite me anymore, and no claw-crossing?"

As soon as Hiccup had removed his fingers, Toothless went all limp and floppy.

"T-t-toothless so w-w-weak . . . can't sniff when he's so w-w-weak . . . ," he moaned pathetically.

"RIGHT," said Hiccup, "you can have the

other half of the mackerel if you BEHAVE FROM NOW ON."

"Okay, then," grumbled Toothless, shaking his wings. "T-t-toothless Daydreams such g-g-g-good sniffers they don't have to p-p-practice, but OKAY."

Hiccup and Fishlegs scraped the disgusting mess of the rest of the mackerel from the bottom of Stoick's bed — Stoick was NOT going to be pleased — and fed it to Toothless, as well as a small haddock pie and three or four oysters.

"He won't be able to FLY at this rate," said Fishlegs.

They set off into the hills and bogs of Berk, Toothless whining the whole way, "C-c-carry me, c-c-carry me, my w-w-wings ache. . . . Are we n-n-nearly there yet?"

Berk was always a wild-looking place, tree-less and boggy, heather-blown and fern-filled. And, of course, it was practically always raining, anything from a light, persistent drizzle to a drenching downpour. (There are twenty-eight words that mean "rain" in the Hooligan language.)

But if you like your landscapes bleak and dramatic, Berk was attractive in its own way, and this was now spoilt by the great muddy holes the Hooligans were digging everywhere, ever since they had become obsessed with hunting for treasure.

What with avoiding the holes, and wading through waist-high gorse and bracken, it took the boys an hour or so even to get up into the hills to practice. And by the time they got there, Horrorcow had fallen into such a deep sleep on Fishlegs's shoulder it was impossible to wake her.

Hiccup brought out an old gold bracelet of his mother's for Toothless to sniff.

"That's the smell you're looking for," he said.

"N-n-no problem," said Toothless. "Easy-p-p-peasy..."

After two hot and breathless hours of running around after Toothless and digging where he said he could sniff something, the boys surveyed what they had found.

1 turnip
3 rabbits (couldn't catch them)
1 small broken spoon

Um . . . that's it, really.

Hiccup shook his head mournfully. "It's not good, is it?"

"Not good? NOT GOOD??" exclaimed a jeering voice behind them. "It's *pathetic,* that's what it is."

Hiccup turned round, and there was Snotlout, laughing so hard Dogsbreath had to hold him upright.

"I mean, a VEGETABLE and a PIECE OF CUTLERY?" Snotlout wiped the tears from his eyes. "It's just so brilliantly Useless. . . ."

"Do you really think," tittered Snotlout, once

he had recovered somewhat, "*that* microscopic amoeba," Snotlout pointed at Toothless, "is going to lead you to TREASURE? He couldn't sniff his way to his own bottom."

Toothless bristled angrily.

"But then he's just a mongrel Common or Garden . . . ," scoffed Snotlout.

"Toothless-not-repeat-not-a-Common-or-Garden-D-d-dragon!" howled Toothless. "Toothless VERY RARE breed c-c-called a Toothless Daydream. . . ."

"Now, Fireworm here is a Monstrous Nightmare, one of your pure hunting greenbloods. . . . Look what a REAL hunting dragon can find if she puts her nose to it. . . ." Snotlout reached into a bag slung round his waist and drew out a large silver plate, a dagger with ancient runes winding round the handle and a couple of pretty bead necklaces.

"And that's only an afternoon's work," said Snotlout.

Fireworm purred with pleasure. She shrugged her beautiful, shining, blood-red shoulders.

"To the nose of an aristocrat like myself," she hissed, "the thing was reeking like a week-old haddock."

"Naturally," said Toothless, "if you have a nose the s-s-size of an elephant seal it m-m-makes life easy for you."

Fireworm's nostrils flared furiously. "I have a beautifully proportioned nose," she snapped.

"Now, now, Fireworm," chided Snotlout, who didn't understand Dragonese but knew they were trading insults, "don't let the peasants upset you. Just think of when we get to the Isle of the Skullions and you sniff out the treasure and everybody will know that *I* am the true heir to the Hairy Hooligans. . . . Nice thought, isn't it, Useless?"

Snotlout leant forward, and with the edge of the plate he was holding, pushed Hiccup ve-ry gently backwards until he overbalanced into the mud.

"Har Har Har Har Har!" snorted Snotlout and Dogsbreath, and they sauntered off.

It was very depressing.

All in all, ever since Alvin arrived, Hiccup had been walking around with a sick feeling in his stomach and a prickle of fear crawling spiderishly down the back of his neck.

It wasn't just the thought of the quest to the Isle of the Skullions (although he was already having nightmares about being ripped to pieces by panther-like creatures with teeth like broken glass). It was this feeling that there was something evil, something POISONOUS lurking on the Isle of Berk.

And that something really terrible was going to happen . . . sometime soon. . . .

Does this look like the sort of dragon who would poo in a helmet?

8. MEANWHILE, IN A CAVERN DEEP, DEEP UNDERGROUND

Meanwhile, in a Cavern deep, deep underground, a small Deadly Nadder was crying for its mother.

It had wandered away from its home in the cozy tunnels of the Dragon Nursery, and lost itself in the maze of the Caliban Caves below.

Gradually, as it flapped frantically down wrong turn after wrong turn, the happy hissings and squawkings of its fellow dragons had grown fainter and fainter. For the last hour it had heard only the unhappy echoes of itself as it crept deeper and deeper into the blackness.

What is more, it had the bad luck to stumble into a Cavern inhabited by a gigantic creature who was guarding something precious. This was a far larger and scarier killing machine than a mere Skullion. It was at least a hundred years old, and living for a century in such gloomy depths had done very little for its soul or its brain. It was lonely and bitter, and had a longing for the light, which it had never seen. But most of all it was permanently hungry.

The little Nadder cried for its mother again, and hopped a bit farther forward.

A singularly unattractive sludgy tentacle curled its way around the small dragon and lifted it into the air.

The Creature did something to the Nadder to kill it, something most unpleasant, and the poor little animal let out a last shriek of absolute terror. . . .

And then all was silence.

PIRATE TRAINING PROGRAM TIMETABLE

Name: *Hiccup H. H. III*

	MONDAY	TUESDAY	WEDNESDAY	THURSDAY	FRIDAY
	SWORDFIGHTING AT SEA	*Dont forget gym05 kt!* SHOUTING	FRIGHTENING FOREIGNERS	ROBBERY ●	BASIC BURGLARY
	SWORDFIGHTING AT SEA	DRAGON TRAINING	FRIGHTENING FOREIGNERS	SENSELESS VIOLENCE	BASIC BURGLARY
	[break]	[break]	[break]	[break]	[break]
	SPITTING	ADVANCED RUDERY	WEAPONRY	ADVANCED RUDERY *NOT My favorite.*	BADD SPPELING
	[break]	[break] *w/ Gobber*	[break]	[break]	[break]
	BASIC BURGLARY	BASHYBALL *Yuck*	DRAGON TRAINING	POINTLESS GRAFFITI	SENSELESS VIOLENCE
	FRIGHTENING FOREIGNERS	BASHYBALL *Yuck*	DRAGON TRAINING	POINTLESS GRAFFITI *art lesson*	SENSELESS VIOLENCE
	Homework: SPITTING	ADVANCED RUDERY	WEAPONRY	SENSELESS VIOLENCE	BADD SPPELING HOOMWURK

9. THE ADVANCED RUDERY LESSON IS INTERRUPTED

This jumpy time of waiting and preparing finally came to an end about two weeks later.

It was halfway through one of Gobber's Advanced Rudery lessons in the Great Hall.

Snotlout was in front of the rest of the class, having a Rudery Battle against Tuffnut Junior. Tuffnut Junior was struggling. He was naturally a good-natured boy, and insults were not his strong point.

"You," said Tuffnut Junior, trying to sound sneery, "are a big fat . . . and I mean really, *really* fat . . . BULLY . . . and your granny is a . . . your granny is a . . . your granny is a . . . very naughty person. . . ."

"Oh, for Thor's sake, Tuffnut Junior!" exploded Gobber furiously, tearing his beard out. "This is a *simple* exercise, can't you do better than THAT? Snotlout's granny is a yellow-bellied decrepit old oyster, Snotlout's granny is a barking mad old walrus-head. . . ."

"Wossat????" howled Snotlout, so psyched up for the lesson that he didn't care *who* he attacked.

"No, no, Snotlout," soothed Gobber, "not *really*, I'm just telling Tuffnut . . . you're supposed to think of something **EXTRA VILE** and then spit the words out . . . you show him, Snotlout."

"With pleasure," leered Snotlout. He leaned forward until his nose was just inches away from Tuffnut's. He grabbed Tuffnut around the neck for extra emphasis. His mean little eyes narrowed with menace, his nostrils quivered with temper.

"*You,*" he spat out with savage contempt, "are a cowardly cowering cuttlefish. . . ."

"**BRILLIANT**, Snotlout, **BRILLIANT**," cheered Gobber.

". . . with the heart of a jellyfish, the brains of a plankton and the stink of a barrelful of mackerel heads."

"Oh BRAVO," boomed Gobber, "you go straight to the top of the class. At this rate, Snotlout, you will have no problems whatsoever becoming a pirate, which is more than I can say for the rest of you. . . ."

ETC, ETC, ETC . . .

Hiccup raised his eyes to the heavens. He went on absentmindedly drawing pictures in his Insults Book.

He was unexpectedly interrupted by the arrival of Stoick the Vast, and behind him, smiling charmingly, Alvin the Poor-but-Honest Farmer.

"I apologize for disturbing your lesson, Gobber," beamed Stoick.

"Not at all, not at all," said Gobber.

"But I bring GOOD NEWS. We are about to set out on our glorious QUEST TO THE ISLE OF THE SKULLIONS!!"

There was a short silence, in which Fishlegs turned white as a sheet and made faint moaning noises.

And then everybody else started cheering.

Hiccup put up his hand.

ME
snotlout
help

Name Hiccup H-H. III
Subject Insults Book
Advanced Rudery
Form

Gobber is a girly

I HEERD that. NO YOU DO
wate till I gett yoo
Dogsbreath has a face like a
squashed oyster

If lost please return to:
Hiccup H. Haddock III
Isle of Berk
The Icy Wastes
Norethern Barbaria
Planet Earth   Toothless
The Universe   Endless Space

"What about the Skullions?" he asked.

"I'm glad you asked that," replied Stoick the Vast enthusiastically. "As we all know," he patted Hiccup affectionately on the head, "Skullions are terrifyingly vicious creatures. . . ."

"Savage beyond your wildest dreams," murmured Hiccup.

"BUT," beamed Stoick, "they have not only lost their ability to fly, but also their sense of SIGHT. Indeed, they are guided to their prey almost entirely by smell alone. So it is Alvin's theory that if we BATHE thoroughly before we go — unusual, I know, but you have to suffer to be rich — we should be all right."

Fishlegs put up his hand. "Theory? *Should* be? What you're saying is that Alvin doesn't actually KNOW, and we could find ourselves flat on our backs being chewed to death very slowly by a bunch of ravenous reptiles."

Stoick nodded.

"In which case you shall enter Valhalla a Hero of the Tribe! And may I say here," said Stoick solemnly, "that anyone who dies in the course of his duty shall be awarded a posthumous Black Helmet."

"Oh yippee," murmured Hiccup.

"DEATH OR GLORY!" yelled Stoick the Vast, performing the complicated Hooligan salute, which consists of making a slitting motion across your own throat while letting out a fart like a clap of thunder.

"DEATH OR GLORY!" shouted Gobber the Belch, and eleven of the trainees shouted fanatically, "DEATH OR GLORY!" and made the salute back at him.

"OH, not this AGAIN," groaned Hiccup and Fishlegs to themselves.

Stoick and Alvin's plan really was that simple. The Hooligans and dragons had to bathe themselves thoroughly. They had to present themselves the next day at the Great Hall, where Alvin would make sure they passed what Alvin called "the Sniff Test." This consisted of Alvin, who was good at this sort of thing, seeing if he could smell them or not, and the expedition would set off.

Hiccup nerved himself up to talk to his father, never an easy task.

"Father," said Hiccup to Stoick, after he had bathed himself and Toothless very thoroughly indeed.

"Hmmmm?" replied Stoick absentmindedly.

OH, not tHis AGAIN..!

He was attempting to dry off his own dragon, Newtsbreath, in front of the fire.

Newtsbreath was an acne-covered sludge green Gronckle the size of a small lion. He loathed water. It had taken Stoick forty minutes to catch him and dump him in the tub. Now he made a furious lunge at Stoick, grabbing his left forearm between his massive jaws. Stoick laughed merrily and gave him a sharp whack on the nose with the scrubbing brush.

"Now, now, Newtsbreath," chided Stoick, "don't be grumpy."

"I'm worried," continued Hiccup, "that we may be setting out on the wrong quest. Do you really think

we should be looking for treasure? We're quite happy
and peaceful enough without all that money."

Stoick ruffled Hiccup's hair affectionately.

"Don't you see," said Stoick excitedly, "YOU'RE
going to be the one to find this treasure. That's what
the riddle said, 'Only the True Heir can find it.'
It has troubled me for some time that Baggybum
and Snotlout might have their eyes on your throne.
When YOU find the treasure, it will silence them
forever. I'm doing this as much for YOU as for the
gold and the glory, although I do see myself in a pair of
fancy earrings, I must admit. . . ."

"But what if I DON'T find the treasure?" asked
Hiccup.

But Stoick wasn't listening. He had stomped off
to get ready.

"Oh bother," said Hiccup.

Newtsbreath
in the bath

10. THE WORST DAY OF HICCUP'S LIFE SO FAR

At dawn on the day of the Quest, Hiccup got dressed very reluctantly indeed. He buckled on the sword his father had given him, hoping that it wouldn't get in the way too much. He slung a shovel in a sling across his back, where he normally might have carried a bow and arrow. He was so nervous he couldn't eat his porridge.

He finally managed to drag Toothless out of bed and set off towards Hooligan Harbor, where everybody was meeting.

Toothless sat on his shoulder, angrily rubbing sleep out of his eyes with one wing.

"Toothless don't W-W-WANT to go on Quest," he complained. "Is s-s-stupid. Is s-s-silly. Is d-d-dangerous."

Hiccup could not have agreed with him more, but all he said was, "You're going to be all right. YOU'VE got wings. Any Skullions attack you, and you just fly away."

"Yes, but T-t-t-toothless don't like the sight of

85

b-b-blood . . . ," whined Toothless. "You get torn to pieces and Toothless feel s-s-sick. . . ."

"We all have our problems," snapped Hiccup crossly.

Fishlegs was already at the Harbor, looking furious. His dragon, Horrorcow, sat at his feet, chewing quietly.

All the other boys were milling about, their dragons fighting each other or flapping over their heads. Everybody was thoroughly overexcited despite the very real prospect of being eaten alive.

DRAGON ARMOR

head goes in here →

A cape made out of thick, heavy leather to protect the shoulders and chest.

"Who do you reckon would win if a Skullion was to fight a Bloody Crocoraptor in one-to-one combat?" chatted Wartihog.

"Oh, the Skullion would win EVERY TIME," replied Clueless. "No question. My father says the Skullion is one of the most vicious creatures on the planet. It'd just whip out that famous extra-long claw and swipe . . . it'd be Goodnight Crocoraptor. . . ."

DRAGON GLOVE

Worn to protect the hand and Upper arm while Dragon training

"Ah," said Wartihog craftily, "but what if the Skullion had one paw tied behind its back, who would win then?"

"Idiots," fumed Fishlegs. "Idiots!! I'm surrounded by people with seaweed for brains."

Other than the boys, there were about fifty adult pirates in the Skullion landing party, all of Stoick's biggest and finest Warriors. Alvin was cracking jokes, giving out hearty handshakes and patting everybody on the back.

Stoick the Vast was delighted to be setting off on a military operation and marched about yelling orders.

"RIGHT, everybody. Once we've landed we split up into groups of two. We fan out across the island, and we get our dragons to sniff for the treasure. Notice you have all been supplied with a whistle — Gobber, could you demonstrate?"

Gobber blew a sharp blast on the whistle.

"P-e-e-e-e-e-e-e-e-e-ep!"

"Once you hear that noise you will realize that somebody has found the treasure. Make your way towards the sound as quickly as possible so we can all help to carry it back to the ship. REMEMBER, the dragons will be sleeping during the day and it does not matter how much noise you make because the Skullion is stone-deaf. However, do try not to

step on one and don't forget that their sense of smell is
very acute indeed. So once you land on the island,
THERE WILL BE ABSOLUTELY NO FARTING
WHATSOEVER. Is that understood?"

The Warriors nodded solemnly.

"Righto, then," said Stoick. "Death or Glory."

"DEATH OR GLORY!" yelled everybody.

And the Grimbeard's Treasure-Seeking Skullion
Landing Party climbed aboard the good ship *Lucky
Thirteen* to set sail for the Isle of the Skullions.

Dogsbreath the Duhbrain "accidentally" bumped
into Hiccup as they climbed in and knocked him on
to the floor of the boat, where Snotlout trod on him.

"Clumsy me," grinned Snotlout, swinging the
Flashcut in a nonchalant fashion. "Good luck, Useless."

Lucky Thirteen set off slowly from the harbor through an ominous thick fog hanging heavily over the whole of the Inner Isles. It was difficult to see more than six feet ahead.

After three or four hours they caught sight of the Isle of the Skullions looming spookily through the mist. And Hiccup's immediate thoughts were, in no particular order, "Let's go home! Turn around! ABANDON SHIP!"

"Don't sweat," he told himself. "Skullions can smell sweat." But he could feel himself getting hotter and hotter with seasickness and fright as the island drew closer and closer. . . .

In fact, even the bravest and most chatty of the Hooligans fell silent as they sailed deeper and deeper into waters their Tribe had been forbidden to enter for hundreds and hundreds of years.

For the Isle of the Skullions was a very sinister place.

The black cliffs in their odd pillar-like formations and the bloody bright-red earth seemed to whisper the word, "Death."

All around there were crazy towers of limpet shells stacked up in piles perilously high, like so many fantastic sculptures. Being unable to fly or swim, the Skullions were imprisoned on the island. They had long ago finished off any small mammals, reptiles or birds that had once lived there. For years they had had

to exist on shellfish, the limpet in particular because
it was so plentiful.

There was no sign of life anywhere. No rabbits,
mice or other scuttly creatures running around the
hillsides. No birds calling from the cliff tops. Nor were
there any signs of the Skullions, either. There *were*,
however, worryingly enormous holes dotted all over
the landscape.

"Those must be their burrows," thought Hiccup.

They were larger than any burrows Hiccup had
ever seen before. Some of the holes were as big as the
front door of the Great Hall.

"They must be somewhere down there," thought Hiccup, swallowing hard.

Because there were no animals or birds, and no winds on such a calm day, there was an eerie silence.

Except, that is, for one terrifying sound.

Imagine the set-your-teeth-on-edge screech of chalk scratching on a blackboard multiplied hundreds of times over. It was the sort of noise you might get if you were sharpening a thousand knives on a thousand stones, but it was far more excruciating than that. It sent all of Hiccup's nerve endings wincing and jangling, even as he realized what the horrible rhythmic scritch-scratch was.

It was the sound of the Skullions sharpening that extra-long claw of theirs on a rock deep within their burrows. This was a practice Hiccup knew about, but had never actually heard in real life before, called "sleep-sharpening."

Hiccup took a deep breath. "Well, at least we know they're asleep," he thought.

The Hooligans had to row three-quarters of the way around the island before they found a place where the boats could land safely. It was a wide-open bay, again with that strange blood-red sand.

Alvin stood up to make a speech.

Every dragon on the boat hissed and growled warningly as he spoke.

"I wanted to wish everybody the best of Viking luck," he said, smiling smoothly and easily. "To my great, great sadness, I will not be able to join you on this part of the Quest. Nothing would give me greater pleasure than to risk my life in this glorious enterprise. But even though I have washed thoroughly I am afraid my smell is so strong to dragons that it might put the whole operation in jeopardy. I shall just stay here and look after the boats."

"And it was all h-h-his idea in the first place!" said Toothless, outraged, in Hiccup's ear. "S-see what Toothless means? An Outcast AND a c-c-coward...."

Stoick patted his friend sympathetically on the back. "Very noble of you, Alvin," he whispered loudly. (It was difficult not to whisper even though the creatures had no ears to hear with.) "I'm sorry you have to miss out on the fun. Okay, men, find yourself a partner, fan out across the island and if nobody finds anything at all, we'll meet back here in an hour."

Fireworm was in a frenzy of excitement as soon as they landed. She had clearly scented

95

something already, and was dying to follow it up, her tail thrashing, whimpering and dribbling with her eagerness to be off.

"Now, no following US," grinned Snotlout, aiming a kick at Hiccup as he and Dogsbreath hurried after her.

Hiccup and Fishlegs stood looking at Toothless, but Toothless was showing no such joy at the task ahead. He sat calmly on the sand licking his tail in a thoughtful fashion. Fishlegs's dragon, Horrorcow, had already fallen asleep under a bench on the boat, so SHE was going to be no help.

"Can you sniff anything?" whispered Hiccup hopefully.

Toothless sniffed.

"POOH," he said in disgust. "Lergified limpets and s-s-sunbaked Skullions ... Y-Y-Y-Y-YUCKY. L-l-l-l-let's get out of here."

"No, no, no," whispered Hiccup. "Treasure. Gold. Jewels. That sort of thing."

And he added craftily, "I'm sure a TOOTH-LESS DAYDREAM like yourself can sniff far better than a mere Monstrous Nightmare."

Toothless swelled with indignation as he

96

remembered the nerve of that Fireworm creature.
He sniffed some more.

"Toothless HAS got a slight c-c-c-cold," he said with dignity, "but that doesn't b-b-bother us aristocrats. There M-M-MIGHT be something coming from over there."

And he waved a claw vaguely towards the left.

So Hiccup drew his too-big sword, and they set off, keeping a sharp eye out for any Skullions that might be awake.

They waded through waist-high ferns and endless heather, much as they might have done on Berk. At one point they passed a GIGANTIC footprint in the mud. Hiccup knelt down to examine it.

"Woden preserve us," he murmured. "This means the Skullion is about TWICE as big as we previously thought."

"No question that it'd beat the Bloody Crocoraptor in one-to-one combat, then," said Fishlegs, unable to stop himself from laughing hysterically. "Oh, this is great, on top of everything else, I'm going CRAZY."

Hiccup was feeling nervous about so many things it was difficult to concentrate on which worry

97

to worry about most. He HAD to find the treasure. It was bad enough being the worst swordfighting trainee EVER, but if he didn't find this treasure that the Heir was supposed to find, then his father was going to be really disappointed. Hiccup hated disappointing his father, even though he had lots of practice at it.

And what if SNOTLOUT found the Treasure? Hiccup went cold and clammy at the thought.

He looked doubtfully at Toothless, who was hitching a ride perched on Fishlegs's shovel. He had shown no promise whatsoever when they had been practicing on Berk.

But Toothless had triumphed in a crisis before. When Hiccup was swallowed by a Seadragonus Giganticus Maximus, Toothless had flown up the Monster's nostril, causing him to sneeze, and saving Hiccup's life. So he DID have hidden and surprising depths.

Maybe he was a hidden Sniffer as well as a hidden Hero. Maybe he really HAD caught a whiff of something. . . . Maybe . . .

Toothless thoughtfully picked his nose, examined the booger on the end of one talon, and swallowed it. He suddenly flapped off the spade and started leading the little procession in a worryingly aimless fashion. At one point he led them in a pointless circle. At another Hiccup stopped him in the nick of time before he woke up all the Skullions by doing a poo. Finally he settled on a small grassy patch at the top of a little hill. He sat down and scratched his ear.

"C-c-could be here," he said absentmindedly.

Hiccup's heart beat a little quicker.

"Here?" he asked. Toothless nodded in an offhand way. The boys took out their shovels and, forgetting about the Skullions in their excitement, started to dig.

After about ten minutes of shoveling, they hit on an underground cache of limpet shells.

"Frittering Freya," said Fishlegs. "These Skullions eat a LOT of limpets. I bet this whole HILL is made out of limpets. I bet this whole ISLAND is made out of limpets. . . ."

Hiccup's shovel hit on something hard and large and heavy just below the surface. Hiccup held his breath. He prodded again. Yes, it was definitely hard and heavy.

"I think I've got something here," he whispered.

Toothless leapt up and down in excitement.

"T-T-TREASURE! T-T-TREASURE!" he chanted. "You going to be a Hero! And T-t-toothless the Hero's Dragon! You going to be . . ."

Hiccup reached down, caught an edge of the hard object and, struggling with both hands, p-u-l-l-e-d out of the earth . . .

The most gigantic limpet shell anyone had ever seen.

At exactly the same moment as Hiccup sat down suddenly, gazing at the limpet, there was the faint, clear sound of a whistle being blown not far away.

"P-e-e-e-e-e-e-e-e-e-e-ep!"

"Useless," said Hiccup, staring at the limpet. "I really am USELESS. This is the second time the Gods have sent me a sign. The first time they sent me a minuscule dragon three times smaller than anyone else's. . . ."

"Thank you," said Toothless, staring down into the hole. "D-d-d-don't understand it. Really DID smell m-m-m-metal. . . ."

". . . THIS time they send me a gigantic limpet."

"It's the most enormous limpet I've ever seen," said Fishlegs in awe. "I think you may have discovered a whole new species."

"Oh brilliant," said Hiccup sarcastically, "*that'll* impress the Tribe. They're all such NATURE LOVERS."

He was feeling very black.

"A limpet," said Hiccup, "HOWEVER big it is, is only ever a limpet. It's not TREASURE, is it? I never heard of a saga where the Hero discovers a new type of mollusk. . . ."

1o1

"Meanwhile," Hiccup continued, "I hear that the REAL Heir to the Hairy Hooligan Tribe has found the treasure. PLEASE don't let it be Snotlout."

Hiccup repeated this to himself over and over again as they trudged towards the continuous noise of the whistle.

"Please don't let it be Snotlout, PLEASE don't let it be Snotlout, please, *please*, PLEASE don't let it be Snotlout. . . ."

11. THE TREASURE OF GRIMBEARD THE GHASTLY

Of course it was Snotlout who had found the treasure.

There he stood, chest stuck out, nostrils flaring, a big fat smile on his smug face. Fireworm, his dragon, had blown up to nearly twice her size with pride.

He was surrounded by a crowd of Vikings, who were giving him the Hooligan Hoorah: "SNOT-LOUT SNOT-LOUT SNOT-LOUT, UGH UGH UGH."

Snotlout grinned even more widely when he saw Hiccup trudging up, trying to look inconspicuous (difficult when you are attended by a friend carrying a gigantic limpet).

"Look what *I've* found, Hiccup," drawled Snotlout.

Snotlout had found a large wooden chest, very battered and scuffed and thoroughly gnawed by Skullions. It had the words **"PROPERTY OF GRIMBEARD THE GHASTLY. DO NOT OPEN"** written on it in large golden letters.

Hiccup sighed. No chance of it NOT being the treasure, then.

"Righto then," said Stoick, rubbing his hands together in a businesslike fashion. "Let's open it."

Hiccup forgot about shutting up and keeping a low profile.

"Father," he whispered urgently, "we can't open it here. Look, it says 'DO NOT OPEN' on the front. Remember what happened last time?"

"NONSENSE," bellowed Stoick, who had never been more disappointed by his son. Why hadn't HE found the treasure? WHAT was his odd-looking friend doing carrying that ridiculously large shell?

Now Baggybum was going to start suggesting that Snotlout was the rightful Heir to the Tribe, and then Stoick would have to shut him up by fighting him, and it was all Hiccup's fault.

"Of course we open it NOW. What's the point of looking for treasure if you can't open the box when you find it?"

"Please," pleaded Hiccup, "you don't think a cunning old pirate like Grimbeard the Ghastly is going to leave a box lying around without there being some sort of trick to it? It'll be BOOBY-TRAPPED. Look what happened when Alvin opened the coffin in the first place — it chopped off his hand — and then

when we opened it later everybody nearly died
of fright. . . ."

Stoick finally lost his temper with his son.

"**WHO** is in charge here, anyway?" he roared.
"*I* am the Chief of the Hairy Hooligans, not you,
you small boy."

Hiccup flinched.

"Those were coincidences, not BOOBY TRAPS.

And I am not going to lug a great heavy box like this one all the way home only to find it's full of stones."

Stoick's eyes were already bright with a strange greedy light that Hiccup had never seen before.

"Good point, Chief," said Gobber the Belch. "May I?" Gobber swung his axe way over his head and brought it down on the chains wrapped around the box, snapping them in two.

"Snotlout should open it, as HE found it," said Baggybum the Beerbelly.

Stoick sighed. "Okay then," he said.

Snotlout proudly stepped forward. This was his big moment.

He shot a nasty look at Hiccup.

"Not a good idea, NOT a good idea, NOT A GOOD IDEA," said Hiccup and Fishlegs to themselves as Snotlout reached out tattooed muscly arms towards the box. . . .

"Not a good idea, N-N-N-NOT a good idea, NOT A G-G-GOOD IDEA," said Toothless, closing his eyes as Snotlout slowly lifted up the lid. . . .

c-r-e-e-e-e-e-e-e-e-e-e-e-e-e-a-k . . .

12. ESCAPE FROM THE ISLE OF THE SKULLIONS

The chest was not full of stones.

It was full to the brim with a gorgeous treasure. Strings of jewels, golden cups, objects more dazzlingly bright than anything the Hooligans had ever seen before.

"Is it s-s-s-safe to look n-n-n-ow?" asked Toothless, still with his eyes shut.

Hiccup opened his eyes. "I think so," he said uncertainly.

He had drawn his sword as Snotlout opened the chest, and now he peered in.

"It seems," he said suspiciously, "it seems to be just a box full of treasure."

"OF COURSE it is," said Stoick. "What did I tell you? No BOOBY TRAPS. You have too much imagination, my boy. Sometimes you have to leave things to the experience of your elders and betters."

Snotlout had already reached in and drawn out a truly magnificent sword, the scabbard richly decorated with dragons, skulls and the waves of an angry sea.

THAT was a sword fit for a Pirate King. It made the soft hiss of a serpent as Snotlout gently drew it out of the scabbard, and as the sunlight glinted on the still-bright, cruel blade, you could see how bitingly sharp it was, even after all these years underground.

On the handle was a furious portrait of Thor the Thunderer with a tangled seaweedy beard, and across the blade was a zigzag lightning pattern in a lighter silver.

"The Stormblade . . . ," breathed Baggybum the Beerbelly.

It was, indeed, the Stormblade, Grimbeard the Ghastly's famous sword, with which he had ruled over the entire Inner Isles in such a ruthless fashion.

As Snotlout waved it gently to and fro, it seemed to give off a fierce, hungry light of its own.

Gently, Stoick reached over and took it from his nephew.

"MINE, I think you'll find," said Stoick calmly. "The Stormblade belongs to the CHIEF of the Hairy Hooligans, and to him ALONE."

There was a crafty, greedy look in his eye as he threw aside his own sword and took hold of the Stormblade.

Toothless wrinkled his snout and sniffed.

"What's that s-s-s-s-smell?"

"What smell?" asked Hiccup.

"THAT smell," replied Newtsbreath, making a face.

Hiccup looked across at Fireworm, the greatest sniffer of them all. The normally flame-red dragon was drooping on Snotlout's shoulder, an extraordinary shade of pale green.

"Suffering scallops!" shouted Hiccup.

"The Skullions!!! SHUT THE BOX!" and he launched himself at the box lid, trying to shut it.

"The boy's gone crazy," said Baggybum the Beerbelly, easily preventing Hiccup from shutting it by holding it open with one massive forefinger.

"Crazy with jealousy," sneered Snotlout.

"SHUT THE BOX! SHUT THE BOX! SHUT THE BOX!" yelled Hiccup, struggling in Baggybum's arms.

"Now, now, my boy," said Stoick, irritated, but trying to soothe his son, "you can find some treasure NEXT time, I'm sure. We're quite safe, the Skullions can't see us or hear us. . . ."

"But they can SMELL us!" shouted Hiccup. "GRIMBEARD HAS BOOBY-TRAPPED THE BOX WITH A SMELL THAT WILL WAKE THE SKULLIONS!!!"

"What do you mean, smell us?" asked Stoick. He gave an

experimental sniff. Now the stench was so strong even the humans were noticing it. Fireworm had already thrown up in the heather. All the Hooligans started sniffing, and there it was, an unmistakable reek of rotting fish and long-dead walrus . . . with perhaps a hint of month-old crabmeat.

"POOH," murmured the Hooligans, their attention wandering from the treasure.

"SHUT . . . THE . . . BOX!" yelled Hiccup, purple in the face from fury at their stupidity. Light dawned on Stoick the Vast's stupid countenance.

"Ahhhhh . . . I see what you mean. . . . SHUT THE BOX. Quickly, quickly!" At last he realized the urgency of the situation and shut the box, sitting on it for good measure.

But it made no difference.

The smell was getting stronger by the minute, an unimaginably horrid stench.

If the Skullions caught just one WHIFF of that horrible smell, it wouldn't take long for them to wake up and . . . the thought was too awful to contemplate.

And then Hiccup realized that the awful scritch-scratch of the sleep-sharpening had stopped . . . and that meant . . . that meant . . .

"R-R-R-U-U-U-U-U-U-U-U-U-N!" shouted
Hiccup.

At exactly the same moment Fireworm shrieked,
"D-E-S-E-R-R-R-R-R-R-R-R-R-T!"

"Let's get out of here," said Stoick the Vast. He
and Gobber the Belch carried the box together. The
Hooligans didn't need the order. They were already
running as fast as they could towards the beach
where the boats were. . . .

"Leave the box here, Father," panted Hiccup as he jogged along beside his father. "They'll go for the box, not us."

"NO WAY," said Stoick, his eyes still shining with that glow Hiccup hadn't seen before. "Think of Alvin's disappointment. Besides, this is my chance for GREATNESS," he huffed, knocking over a big tower of limpets as he blundered along.

"You are great ALREADY, Father," urged Hiccup, "you don't need this treasure. . . ."

But Stoick wouldn't leave it behind.

As they passed the burrows Hiccup could begin to hear horrible snuffling noises coming from inside.

He ran a bit faster.

His heart pounding in terror, he bounded through the heather and crashed through the ferns, at one point falling flat on his face.

The smell was now so strong that it was becoming visible, drifting out of the dents and cracks Gobber had made in the chest in a thick greeny-yellow vapor.

The cliffs of the beach were in sight. They had passed the last mound of Skullions. Maybe they would make it after all.

And then Hiccup heard a noise that made his stomach turn double-somersaults in terror. The noise of animals like big dogs or lions padding behind him, bounding through the heather.

"R-r-r-r-r-r-run!" shrieked Toothless, who was flying three or four feet above Hiccup's head.

Hiccup, Fishlegs, Stoick and Gobber were trailing behind the others, Hiccup and Fishlegs because they were not fast runners, Stoick and Gobber because they were hampered by the box they were carrying.

"So they'll get us first," thought Hiccup.

The Skullions were now so close behind them that they could hear the horrible snotty snuffling noises they were making in their noses and the clicking of their teeth.

Hiccup reached the brow of the dunes and launched himself off it in a huge jump onto the sand below. He landed okay but tripped over his too-large Stretchapoint sword. He rolled over onto his back to look up at the ghastly sight of a gigantic slobbering Skullion, claws outstretched, leaping right on top of him. Its great head was just inches above Hiccup's face.

It was the most dreadful thing Hiccup had
ever seen, and it would give him nightmares until
he was an old, old man. It was a face that wasn't
a face, no eyes and ears, just that vast nose and
slobbering mouth, punctuated by sparkling silver teeth.
Black saliva dripped down onto Hiccup's face in a
disgusting dribble. The Skullion was holding him
down with one clawed paw, while he sniffed down the
rest of his body, searching for the tendon in his ankles,
the sunlight glinting on that one ludicrously
overgrown talon. . . .

Hiccup fumbled for his sword, but the
Stretchapoint had fallen out of reach.

Hiccup opened his mouth to shout for help,
but no noise came out.

"Help me," he mouthed soundlessly.
"HELP ME."

Somebody appeared from nowhere, grabbed
the Skullion around the throat and killed it with one
blow from his sword.

It was Stoick the Vast.

The strange grip the treasure had on Stoick
loosened as soon as he saw his son's life was in danger.

He left Baggybum the Beerbelly to carry the

chest to the ship. He was holding the Stormblade in his right hand and an axe in his left.

"MOVE!!!" yelled Stoick the Vast.

Hiccup moved. He stumbled across the sand.

He could hear more of the creatures bounding after him.

"I'm not . . . going . . . to . . . make it . . . to the boats in time," he thought to himself.

There was a hollow tree trunk sunk into the sand in front of him.

"Climb under the t-t-tree! Climb under the tree!" screeched Toothless.

Hiccup scrambled under it in the nick of time. He could hear a Skullion's jaws clanging together just as he pulled his ankle through the dip in the sand below the tree.

The Skullion was too large to follow him but it pushed its revolting quivering nose through the gap and it started to gnaw at the wood around the hole.

Hiccup grabbed a bone lying on the ground and shoved it as hard as he could up one gigantic nostril.

The Skullion fell back with a howl of anguish.

There was a sickening crash from above as a Skullion landed on top of the tree . . . and then another . . . and another. . . . Hiccup could hear horrible scratchings as they worried away with their teeth, trying to break through the wood.

Way above that, Toothless was screaming continuously, "H-h-help! Help! H-H-H-H-HELP!"

Hiccup swiped at another nose appearing at the hole. . . .

All around him at the edges of the tree trunk he could hear the scrabbling sound of creatures digging through the sand.

It was only a question of time before one of them broke through. . . .

Through a crack at eye level Hiccup could see his father fighting his way towards him up the beach. His dragon hadn't deserted him. Noble Newtsbreath was recklessly tearing into the back of a Skullion three times larger than himself that was about to leap at Stoick.

C-R-U-N-C-C-C-C-C-C-C-C-CH!

A Skullion talon pierced the tree trunk, so close to Hiccup that it grazed his chest as it went through.

The head and shoulders of the Skullion appeared in the gaping hole the talon had made. It opened its jaws so wide Hiccup could see right down its black throat.

Hiccup screamed and fell backwards.

Just as the creature lunged forwards to kill him, Hiccup was grabbed around the ankle by one of Stoick's hairy hands, and pulled back through the hole he had climbed in.

Stoick dragged him out, and lifted him up.

"Put your arms up!" bellowed Stoick.

Newtsbreath, hovering overhead, took hold of Hiccup's arms with his talons and carried him up into the air. Toothless grabbed one leg, struggling to help.

Newtsbreath spread out his great wings to their fullest extent.

The Skullions chased after them as they flew, leaping up to bite at Hiccup like dogs after a tidbit. Newtsbreath groaned with the strain of trying to get enough height to keep Hiccup out of range of their snapping jaws.

Every now and then, the effort became too much

for him, and to Hiccup's terror, he
plunged suddenly downwards towards
the beach. There was one very close
call when Hiccup swung his body out
of the way just in time as one of the
monsters made a tremendous leap
and nearly took his legs off at the knee.

By the time they got to the sea,
Newtsbreath's strength had gone,
and Hiccup's ankles were dragging
in the water.

But they were safe.

Skullions cannot swim, and
they loathe the water.

A few more beats of Newtsbreath's
wings, and he dropped Hiccup sprawling on
the deck of the *Lucky Thirteen*. He then
whirled round wearily, and flapped back
to try and help his Master.

Stoick was doing surprisingly well without his help, considering he was fighting a lone battle against increasing numbers of Skullions. Normally, this would have resulted in one dead Chief in about ten seconds flat. You have to remember that Stoick was forty and very, very fat.

But with the Stormblade in his hand, Stoick seemed to have been transformed.

He was awesome.

Yelling the spine-chilling Hooligan Yell, eyes crazy with bloodlust, he performed the Fighting-Against-Superior-Numbers Maneuver with spectacular success.

This is a highly complicated Pirate Fighting Skill that only the most coordinated and brilliant fighters can carry out.

The pirate takes the Double-Headed Supa-Axe in his left hand and whirls it around his head in a continuous circle that the enemies are unable to penetrate without getting their heads chopped off. At the same time, with the right hand the pirate lunges out of the defensive circle with his sword to attack the enemy.

As you can imagine if you have ever tried to rub your stomach with one hand while patting your head with the other, this Attacking-While-Defending Skill can only be carried out by the most brilliant and coordinated of Vikings.

Skullion after Skullion fell down dead around Stoick as he walked slowly forwards. But a continuous shining wave of the Creatures had poured onto the beach and were cutting off his route to the boats. It seemed impossible that he could make it through the sheer mass of them all, and Newtsbreath, though flying as hard as he could, was still too far away to be any help.

And then, to the complete astonishment of the watching Hooligans, their corpulent, creaky old Leader leapt onto the **BACK** of the nearest Skullion. The creature madly twisted and bucked, trying to throw him off, but Stoick held on grimly, gripping with his powerful thighs alone, so that he could reach down to right and left, dispatching Skullions with sword and axe.

He cut his way through the mob, riding the maddened beast right into the sea, for all the world as if he were astride an ancient old broken-in Dragon Steed. When the Creature finally bucked him off in the shallows, he turned the fall into a belly flop

forwards, checked for a moment to stow away the sword and the axe, and swam like fury for the boat.

The whole wide bay, and the immediate horizon, was now filled with thousands and thousands of these beasts from hell. It was like a vision out of your worst nightmare.

But the Skullions stopped at the water's edge, and stayed there howling and shrieking furiously. So angry were they that they started turning on the weaker members of their pack, and a few of the creatures were ripped to pieces in front of Hiccup's eyes.

The Hooligans cheered and cheered and cheered.

Stoick was very pleased with himself.

He acknowledged the frantic applause, wiped the blood off the Stormblade onto his shirt, and kissed the clean blade.

And then he threw back his hairy head and ROARED like an animal, and so wild did he look with the sword in his hand and the blood on his shirt that Hiccup barely recognized his own father.

13. THE TREASURE

The graze on Hiccup's chest was actually deeper than he had realized in the terror of the moment. It would leave a scar that would stay with him for the rest of his life as a reminder of a morning spent on the Isle of the Skullions.

And his right arm was dislocated from the strain of hanging from the talons of Newtsbreath. Gobber put it back in its socket (a very painful process, as Gobber was not the most tender of nurses) and tore a strip off his shirt to make Hiccup a sling for it.

The Hooligans gave themselves a couple of minutes to pat each other on the back and celebrate, before grabbing the oars again. They were eager to leave the spooky Isle of the Skullions far, far behind them. It wasn't until they were within sight of the friendly cliffs of Berk that they felt safe enough to ship their oars, and let the *Lucky Thirteen* drift for a while in calm but misty seas while they investigated their prize.

When Stoick lifted the lid of the box again, the smell had nearly gone. But underneath the treasure there was a scattering of greenish-yellow crystals which appeared to be smoking slightly, and they still gave off that rotten-egg stench. These were what Grimbeard had used to booby-trap the box — as soon as they came into contact with the air they let off their smell, which then alerted the Skullions.

A very effective and deadly defense of his treasure.

And WHAT a treasure it was . . . Alvin could not speak for at least three minutes. He just stood there, eyes popping, picking up object after object and stroking it, letting his hands run lovingly through the coins.

"Of course, ten percent of this treasure shall be yours, Alvin," boomed Stoick the Vast, sticking his belly out in pride at his own generosity.

"You are *tooooo* kind, dearest Stoick," murmured Alvin, when he could say anything at all.

"Hang on an oyster-catching minute," interrupted Baggybum the Beerbelly. "Firstly, I want it acknowledged that SNOTLOUT found this treasure."

"Acknowledged," said Stoick the Vast reluctantly.

Hiccup knew he should be thankful to be alive, but he was unspeakably miserable. He knew what all this was going to mean. Hiccup, although the son of the Chief, was not the True Heir to the Hairy Hooligans. The True Heir was Snotlout, who had always been bigger, faster and more brilliant than Hiccup at everything.

"Secondly," continued Baggybum, "as the FINDER OF THE TREASURE, technically it belongs to MY SON Snotlout, and I don't know whether Snotlout feels like giving away any of it to some stranger. . . ."

"He definitely doesn't," grinned Snotlout.

Stoick the Vast banged shut the treasure chest. He lifted Baggybum the Beerbelly clear off the ground by the front of his shirt, which was quite some feat considering Baggybum the Beerbelly was about the size of a killer whale who hadn't had much exercise recently.

"I AM THE CHIEF OF THIS TRIBE!" roared Stoick the Vast. "I LAUNCHED THIS EXPEDITION TO FIND THE TREASURE OF GRIMBEARD THE GHASTLY AND THIS TREASURE BELONGS TO ME AND ME ALONE!"

Baggybum the Beerbelly gave Stoick a quick jab in the kidney, which made Stoick drop him, sharpish. He yelled right back in Stoick's face:

"WELL, MAYBE YOU'VE BEEN CHIEF
OF THIS TRIBE A LITTLE TOO LONG, BIG
BROTHER! MAYBE THIS IS A SIGN FROM THE
GODS THAT IT'S TIME YOU RETIRED. WHAT
DID THAT PROPHECY SAY ABOUT THE HEIR
FINDING THE TREASURE? IF MY SON IS
THE HEIR, MAYBE THAT JUST MAKES ME
THE CHIEF OF THE TRIBE INSTEAD OF YOU!!!"

"NO!" yelled Stoick, stamping his foot. "I'M THE CHIEF!"

"ARE NOT!"

"AM TOO!"

They had grabbed each other by the shoulders and were carrying out a Staring Contest, the horns on their helmets locked together like a couple of rutting stags.

"Neff off," said Stoick, with quiet and sinister emphasis.

"No, YOU neff off," replied Baggybum.

"No, YOU neff off."

"YOU!"

"YOU!" etc. etc. etc.

While all this was going on, nobody noticed Alvin doing something rather strange.

When the *Lucky Thirteen* sailed into easy flying distance of the cliffs of Berk, most of the dragons had flown off back to the Hooligan Village, for food and rest. The only one who had remained on the *Lucky Thirteen* was Toothless. Toothless, who was a lazy little creature, considered this too far to fly. And he had caught himself a couple of nice plump mackerel on the way. So there he still was, on the deck, watching the fight with interest.

For some strange reason of his own, Alvin picked up a heavy empty barrel. He placed it over the excited little dragon, trapping him underneath.

He then interrupted the fight between Stoick and Baggybum.

"Now, now," said Alvin soothingly, "little clams in their shells agree. This should be a JOYFUL moment, the beginning of a glorious new era for the Hooligan Tribe. There is plenty of treasure for all of you. I propose a toast to celebrate the finding of the treasure."

The Hooligans cheered, hoping to get over a difficult moment. Gobber and Hugefarts pulled Stoick and Baggybum apart, because otherwise they were clearly prepared to stand there all day. Some of the other Hooligan Warriors handed out black-currant wine for the toast.

Stoick the Vast drew the Stormblade. He had already decked himself out in some fancy earrings from the treasure chest.

"Half-wits and HEROES," he shouted. "We,

a small band of unbeatable barbarians, are about to become the center of a New Empire, an Empire to rival Rome in her glory days! With this treasure," Stoick lifted his cup of black-currant wine, his eyes glittering, "the Hairy Hooligans shall become INVINCI —"

14. THE DAY TAKES A TURN FOR THE WORSE

Stoick never finished the word "invincible" because halfway through he was grabbed around the neck by an enormous wild-eyed individual and a not very clean knife was held to his neck. So the word ended up more like "INVINCI-*ugh-ugh-ugh*," as Stoick choked and his eyes popped.

All around the rowing benches every Hooligan aboard had been grabbed from behind and knives were held at every throat.

The Hooligans' nerves were still jangling from the flight from the Skullions. And they had been so busy arguing that they hadn't spotted a small sleek boat sneaking up through the mist and drawing alongside the *Lucky Thirteen*. A boat named the *Hammerhead* with a sail curved like a shark's fin and a red skull and crossbones painted on the side. A boat packed to the brim with OUTCASTS.

They were not a pretty crew, despite their height, and their handsome red hair, and their gorgeous clothes, and every kind of golden ornament. Many had scars carved into their faces. One or two were without a nose or an ear. Most had filed their teeth into sharp little points, like the teeth of a shark. Even the good-looking ones were disfigured by dark red tattoos, said to be made out of the blood of their enemies. They talked to each other in the most difficult of Viking languages, Outcastese, which sounds very much like the barking of a dog.

The Outcasts had swarmed over the side and crept up behind the Hooligans as they were admiring the Treasure and themselves. Toothless had smelt them, of course. He knew they were coming and he had been going crazy inside the big heavy barrel, shrieking at the top of his voice, "OUTCASTS! R-R-RUN FOR YOUR LIVES, YOU S-S-S-STUPID H-H-HUMANS!!!"

But nobody had heard him.

All in all, this was turning into a very bad day for the Hooligans. Outcasts, like Skullions, are the kind of creature one really hopes one can live a lifetime without bumping into, let alone seeing BOTH of them at close quarters in the space of one morning.

Hiccup did not realize they were Outcasts. But he knew they were Bad Trouble.

His heart started jumping in his chest like a mudskipper as he looked into the terrible face of the man who had Stoick the Vast by the throat. His curly horns were quite three feet high. When he opened his mouth he growled like a dog.

For a whole minute, nobody said a word.

This is Outcastese, and it translates roughly as "Got him! what do we do now, Chief??"

Nobody dared move a muscle. There was no noise at all except for that terrible dog-like growling from the Outcast who was holding Stoick . . . and the sound of Alvin drinking.

There was no knife at Alvin's throat.

Calmly, he finished off the last delicious drops of black-currant wine. Smoothly, he put the cup down.

"I thought that I would provide a — ah — surprise ending to our little journey," said Alvin, with his charming smile. "I DO like surprises, don't you, my dear Stoick?"

Stoick gargled inarticulately.

"Such fun, aren't they?" continued Alvin. "I am so sorry to say, however, that the day of glory for the Hooligan Tribe may be — ah — put off for a while. You see, I feel that I ought to have rather more of the treasure then a mere ten percent. And in case you didn't agree I thought I would bring along some of my relatives to — ah — persuade you to give it up."

Stoick gargled again.

Alvin barked out a few words in Outcastese to Curly Horns, who barked back at him again.

"I have to admit at this point that I have been guilty of a little innocent deception," said Alvin. "My name is not Alvin the Poor-but-Honest Farmer. I am, in fact, His Most Mighty Murderousness Alvin the Treacherous, Great High Chieftain of the Outcast Tribe. I don't know why, but I felt that if I had told you this from the beginning you might not have given me a very warm welcome."

"An OUTCAST?" gasped the Hooligans.

Alvin laughed. "That's right," he said, "an Outcast. Us Outcasts don't always go around on all fours dressed in animal skins, you know. Even *we* are moving with the times." He went over to Stoick and gently removed the Stormblade from Stoick's hand.

137

"MINE, I think," said Alvin.

Alvin unscrewed the claw from his right hand, as Hiccup had seen him do once before. He attached his "sword-holder" contraption in its place, into which he carefully twisted the Stormblade. He screwed it very tightly, so that it was completely steady. And while he did all this, he talked.

"You see, Stoick," said Alvin, "we Barbarian Chieftains are facing a new challenge. We have to fight the creeping forces of Civilization by becoming FIERCER and CRUELER than ever. YOU, Stoick, have GONE SOFT."

"I have NOT!" protested Stoick indignantly.

"Grimbeard the Ghastly would be turning in his grave if he could see you now," tut-tutted Alvin. "You Hooligans have become bungling AMATEURS, all noise and show with no real wickedness to you at all. Now, *I* have worked hard to bring us Outcasts up to date. Outwardly, we now have some of the clothes and the manners of Civilization . . . but inwardly we are tougher and more truly Outcast than we have ever been. We are your REAL PROFESSIONAL PIRATES, heartless, murdering, bloodsucking slave-traders. . . ." Alvin paused for breath.

The Most High and Murderous Alvin the Treacherous

"Talking of which," he then continued, "take your last look at your rather plain little island. . . ." He gestured at the friendly cliffs of Berk. "All of you Hooligans are about to enter the slave trade yourselves, in the very important role of SLAVES."

The Hooligans groaned. There was no worse fate for a proud and independent Viking than to be sold into bondage.

"I am sure you will all make excellent slaves,"
said Alvin kindly, "because you are all very strong, and,
frankly, none too bright. And I do hate to threaten, but
anybody who objects will thoroughly regret it."

An Outcast with no nose stepped forward and
uncurled an ugly black whip from around his waist,
with a handle shaped like a serpent.

Alvin clapped his hands and the Outcasts
began loading the Hooligans onto the deck of
the *Hammerhead*.

"Yup, you shall all be slaves. All that is . . . ," smiled Alvin, ". . . except for you, Stoick."

Curly Horns let Stoick go, and proudly, he stepped forward.

"To Chieftains and their descendants we pay the ultimate sign of respect," said Alvin with just a tiny hint of menace in his voice, "by EATING them."

"But that's CANNIBALISM," said Stoick, shocked.

"I know, I know," sighed Alvin. "It's very old-fashioned of me, but I would lose respect in front of the rest of my Tribe if I dropped ALL the old traditions. . . ."

"But . . . but . . . but . . . but . . . ," blustered Stoick.

"I shall not change my mind, whatever you say," said Alvin gently. "The thing about dinner is, it never wants to be eaten. I mean, you eat PORK, don't you, Stoick?"

"Well, yeees," admitted Stoick.

"There you are then!" said Alvin. "No pig is ever going to VOLUNTEER to be supper, and, thinking of volunteers . . ." Something seemed to be amusing Alvin. He giggled delightedly. "I mentioned that it would not only be Stoick who would receive this, ah . . . honor," said Alvin, "but also his descendants. I know there has been some sort of argument about this recently. The question is," continued Alvin, struggling to keep a straight face, "WHO is the Heir to Stoick the Vast? Could they put up their hand please?"

Strangely enough, Snotlout did not put up his hand at this point.

Instead, he tried to hide behind Dogsbreath the Duhbrain, staring very hard at his bronze-tipped sandals, as if he hadn't quite heard the question.

Hiccup sighed.

He stood right up on the bench so that everyone could see him.

"I," said Hiccup, "I am the Heir to Stoick the Vast."

Stoick smiled a big, proud smile.

For all their manners, the Outcasts whispered a great deal at that. Hiccup didn't have to speak Outcastese to know that they were saying things like: "*That* skinny prawn is the Heir to the Hairy Hooligans???"

Two gigantic Outcasts lifted Hiccup from the bench and set him down next to Stoick the Vast.

Alvin held up the Stormblade. The sword was now just an extension of his arm, like the horn of a narwhal is an extension of its nose.

"It looks as if it has always been there, doesn't it?" said Alvin.

The daylight played across the bolt of lightning motif. Alvin drew a finger across the blade ever so lightly, and blood instantly dropped onto the deck.

"Nice and sharp. This won't take a second," promised Alvin, stepping towards Hiccup.

15. THE BATTLE ON BOARD THE *LUCKY THIRTEEN*

Alvin advanced towards Hiccup, with the Stormblade raised above his head.

Hiccup closed his eyes, waiting for the blow.

But at that moment Toothless finally managed to overturn the barrel he was trapped underneath.

He had been throwing his entire body weight at one side for the past five minutes. At last he made an extra-strong he-*e-e-eave,* the barrel tipped over, and rolled at great speed across the deck with Toothless rumbling round and round inside it . . . and bowled straight into the legs of Alvin the Treacherous . . . who lost his footing and fell over. . . .

Alvin gave an *ooohh* of surprise, the Outcasts

were distracted for one vital second, and Stoick turned round and felled Curly Horns with a good old-fashioned uppercut right under the chin.

From that moment on, there was chaos aboard the *Lucky Thirteen*.

The Hooligans took advantage of their captors' surprise as the swords against their throats were lowered for a moment.

"THIS IS MORE LIKE IT! I'LL TEACH YOU TO SAY THE HOOLIGANS HAVE GONE SOFT!!!!" Stoick let out the Viking War Cry and launched himself on the enemy completely bare-handed. He crashed two Outcasts' heads together, jabbed another in the kidney with his foot, and when that one doubled over in pain, leapfrogged over his back to face another couple of the opposition.

All might not have gone well for him, however, unarmed as he was, if Baggybum the Beerbelly had not come to his aid. The two brothers, who had been fighting each other five minutes earlier, now fought the enemy back-to-back for the rest of the battle.

The "Battle on Board the *Lucky Thirteen*" would be a Saga that the Hooligans would tell their children and grandchildren for many, many years

to come. The military prowess of the Outcast Tribe
was legendary throughout the Viking World. But
the Hooligans were desperate and angry. They were
battling for their FREEDOM itself, and so fought
more wildly, more fiercely, than perhaps they had
ever done before or since.

No fewer than twenty Black Stars* were
awarded to Warriors after the battle was over. No
wonder, for the Pirate Fighting Skills on display on
that occasion were a joy to watch. They were also a
tribute to the old soldier, Gobber, who had taught
most of the Warriors all that they knew. There, on one
corner of the deck, was Nobber Nobrains, performing
the highly skilled maneuver known as the Dance
of the Axes, in which the pirate rapidly juggles two
twirling axes from one hand to the other, hypnotizing
and confusing the enemy, before the pirate lunges
forward for the fatal blow.

Up around the mast were the boys from the
Pirate Training Program, valiantly tackling Outcasts
nearly twice their size, putting into practice all that

---

* The "Black Star" was a medal given to Hooligan Warriors for Outstanding
Bravery in the Field of Combat.

Fishlegs goes
BERSERK

they had learnt during those Swordfighting at Sea lessons.

The behavior of Fishlegs was particularly surprising. As soon as the battle began, he completely lost control, throwing himself at the enemy, shrieking furiously and whirling his sword around his head like a madman.

Vikings call this "going Berserk" and Warriors who do this are revered in Viking society.

You could not imagine a more unlikely candidate for being a Berserk than Fishlegs, but there we are, these things are never predictable.

The Outcasts stayed out of his way, for a Berserk is always respected, even if he is only four foot ten with a squint and a limp and no swordfighting skills whatsoever.

It has to be admitted (reluctantly) that Snotlout fought with spectacular brilliance and bravery. His quick wrist made the Flashcut slip neatly in and out, hither and thither, beautifully performing the Destroyer's Defense, Grimbeard's Grapple, the Final Cut, and many, many more of the subtlest swordfighting skills. In the space of five minutes no fewer than three Outcasts lay dead around him, all much larger and heavier than himself. This is a schoolboy record that stands to this day.

I would love to say that Hiccup fought similarly splendidly. But I can't, because it wouldn't be true. Hiccup had dislocated his arm, remember, and his sword, the Stretchapoint, lay somewhere on the beach at the Isle of the Skullions. But Hiccup did what he could. With his quick left hand he picked a key out of Curly Horns's pocket while he fought Gobber the Belch. He used the key to unlock the chains of four or five Hooligans who had already been bound, ready for slavery, who then joined in the fight with the others.

Toothless created an extra diversion when he spilled out of the barrel, dizzy and confused, and bit the first hairy leg that he saw. Which happened to belong to a grossly fat Outcast, who promptly dropped the flare he had been carrying right in the open barrel of black-currant wine.

And Thor only knows what was IN that black-currant wine, but the entire barrel burst into flames.

The fire raged out of control.

The sail burned furiously, and thick black smoke poured over the deck.

Everybody started jumping off the *Lucky Thirteen* in order to escape the flames.

Stoick belly flopped into the sea, and splashed over to the Outcast boat, the *Hammerhead,* where the pitched battle was continuing. As he climbed over the side of the *Hammerhead,* he turned back to his son and shouted, "Come ON, Hiccup!"

"Your f-f-f-father's right," panted Toothless, "w-w-we should go."

Hiccup hesitated.

Fishlegs was still aboard the *Lucky Thirteen*.

He was in the grip of the Beserk trance, and was following Alvin, sword in hand, hoping to kill him.

The Hammerhead

Alvin had turned back to fetch the treasure.

"FISHLEGS!" yelled Hiccup desperately. "WE'VE GOT TO GET OFF THE BOAT!"

But Fishlegs couldn't hear him.

"FISHLEGS!" shouted Hiccup, hesitating some more. "IF WE DON'T GET OFF NOW WE MAY BE TOO LATE!"

It was already too late.

There was a mighty C-R-E-E-E-E-E-E-E-E-E-A-A-A-K!!!!!! from above and the burning mast crashed into the sea.

Stoick watched in horror from the deck of the *Hammerhead* as the *Lucky Thirteen* flipped over onto its back, trapping Hiccup, Fishlegs, Alvin and Toothless underneath it as it did so.

It then sank before his eyes.

And Stoick knew that this particular part of the ocean, despite being so close to the cliffs, was very, very deep, too deep even for lobster pots.

"HIC-CUP!" yelled Stoick in despair.

He knew that he would never see his son again.

For who could get out of *that* situation alive?

16. AT THE BOTTOM OF THE OCEAN

Hiccup's first thought was that he was going to drown. He was turned over and over in somersault after somersault, down, down, down in such a rush that he felt like his head was bursting. A strange, calm sensation of no longer really caring came over him, and then he was roughly grabbed by the shoulders and dragged coughing and spluttering to the surface of the water and into an air pocket trapped beneath the sinking ship.

The boat was still traveling downwards with such rapidity that Hiccup's ears popped again and again, but at least he could breathe.

"My turn to save YOUR life," gasped Fishlegs.

"Oh yes," said Hiccup sarcastically, once he'd got his breath back, "and I suppose the reason I'm here in the first place is nothing to do with you? If you hadn't gone rushing after Alvin we would be on board the other boat by now. . . . Didn't you hear me shouting at you?"

Fishlegs blushed. "Couldn't hear anything, actually," he mumbled.

"A fine time for us to discover you're a Berserk," grumbled Hiccup.

Fishlegs blushed even deeper. "Do you think that's what it was?" he asked shyly. He was secretly extremely proud that he had these violent hidden depths.

"Yes, I do," said Hiccup. "Anyway, my life isn't exactly SAVED yet, is it? It's not like we're tucked up safely in bed in the Hooligan Village. I mean, where ARE we?"

The boat finally stopped its descent and settled gently on the seabed.

"At the b-b-b-bottom of the ocean," said Toothless as he floated by, crouched in an upturned Outcast helmet like a malevolent eagle sitting on a nest, his eyes glowing like candles. (One of the only interesting features of the Common or Garden dragon is that its eyes light up in the dark.)

"The boat turned over and we seem

to be trapped underneath in some sort of air pocket,"
explained Fishlegs.

Hiccup peered up the length of the upturned
Lucky Thirteen. Sure enough, all the benches were now
the ceiling of what looked like a long, low, barrel-
vaulted hall, with water for a floor. Chairs, oars and
cushions floated by, but as far as he could see or
hear, there was no one else trapped with them, no
furious Outcasts or helpful Hooligans.

"Everyone else must have jumped
off in time," said Fishlegs.

"Hang on a sec," said Hiccup, "somebody
seems to be stuck under a bench down there...."
He dived below the surface, his kicking legs swamping
Fishlegs and Toothless in a small tidal wave.

He was gone for nearly a minute and a half.
When he finally resurfaced, he was holding a very limp
and green Alvin the Treacherous.

"What you saving HIM for?" complained
Toothless. "He a r-r-rat. Toothless kill him, if you
like," he said, cheering up no end, his claws
extending towards the sleeping Alvin.

As if he heard these words, Alvin opened his eyes. His face crumpled up and he cried like a baby.

"My treasure," he cried, "my treasure. Gone, gone, gone. . . ."

"We are not interested in your treasure," said Fishlegs coldly. "What about the fact that not half an hour ago you were about to put the entire Hooligan Tribe into slavery? Not to mention serving up poor old Hiccup here as a starter. If it wasn't for YOUR stupid treasure we could all be sitting in one of Gobber the Belch's classes staring vacantly out of the window while he bangs on about Frightening Foreigners."

"We can still find it," said Alvin urgently, trying to peer into the water below him. "It's down there somewhere, the ground isn't far beneath me. HELP ME everybody, and we shall live like kings. . . ."

"Oh belt up, you madman," snapped Fishlegs.

"We haven't got time," interrupted Hiccup. "This really is our lucky day. Correct me if I'm wrong, but I think this air pocket is getting smaller."

Hiccup was right.

The air pocket was getting smaller.

156

17. HOW BAD COULD THIS DAY GET?

The "ceiling" was definitely nearer to their heads than it had been a few minutes before. It was now just a few inches above the horns on Hiccup's helmet.

There was silence for a second. Alvin's mad eyes swam back into focus again. The only thing that mattered more to him than the treasure was the preservation of his own life.

Hiccup found everyday life rather a trial but was always good in a crisis. "RIGHT," he said, "Toothless, I want you to swim out from under this boat and see whether you think we're too far to swim to the surface. NOW," he added, as Toothless seemed to be taking his time about it.

"Okay, okay," grumbled Toothless, "k-k-k-keep your horns on. . . ."

The little dragon dived underneath the water
and disappeared. He left the Vikings in nearly total
darkness, for without the friendly light of his glowing
eyes it was almost impossible to see. There was an
eerie silence, apart from the lapping of the water
against the sides of the boat, and a faint rushing
noise, which Hiccup was sure was the sound of
the air leaving the air pocket like a leaking balloon.

And indeed, after five minutes the air pocket had
reduced so much that Hiccup's head was squashed
against the wooden "ceiling" of the *Lucky Thirteen,*
and he had to remove his helmet.

Alvin was panicking. "Where is the wretched
reptile?" he hissed, and then choked as water sloshed
into his mouth.

"That wretched reptile," scolded Fishlegs,
as terrified as Alvin but bravely trying not to show it,
"is trying to save *your* wretched life. . . ."

Five minutes more and they had to turn their
heads in order to keep their nostrils clear of the water.
"If Toothless takes any longer," thought Hiccup,
"we're going to drown here in this blackness. . . ."

Two lights flickered in the dark below him.

It was Toothless, swimming up towards them in the nick of time.

"Okay," said Toothless. "Surface t-t-too far away for h-h-h-h-humans . . . but there's a c-c-c-c-cave thingy. . . . F-f-follow Toothless. . . ."

"Just hang on to me, Fishlegs, and kick like crazy," ordered Hiccup, because, of course, Fishlegs could not swim.

Hiccup took a huge breath, *just* before the sea swallowed up the last remains of that air pocket, and dived after Toothless.

He had to swim underneath the rim of the boat, which was resting on some large rocks on the bottom.

He swam out into total darkness, which was very confusing. A little way above him, he could see that Toothless was swimming towards a small hole in the cliff, with light shining out of it. Trying to ignore the panicky feeing of his breath running out, and hampered by Fishlegs gripping on to one leg, he swam as fast as he could towards the hole. Once he had swum into it, he shot upwards through a short tunnel and surfaced in a huge pool of water at the bottom of a gigantic underground cavern, gasping for air.

A second or so later, Alvin emerged to lie in the water beside Hiccup and Fishlegs.

The cavern was huge, and surprisingly light, considering it was so far underground. The eerie green light seemed to be given off by Electricsquirms, a tiny dragon-like creature that glows with phosphorescence. Water rushed down the walls and dripped from the ceiling.

Hiccup was so relieved to be still alive and in the air again that this tomb of a cavern initially seemed like home. It was a while before his scared brain could focus on the fact that they weren't safe yet.

"Right," said Fishlegs, trying not to panic and wringing out his breeches and flapping his arms to get dry. "How are we going to get out of HERE?"

The cavern had some interesting rock

formations, if Hiccup had been in the mood for admiring them. The weird shapes of fossilized dragons were caught in the stone. Some of them were very unusual, extinct species. However, even the discovery of an entire skeleton of the Burrowing Slitherfang, so rare that it was often thought never to have existed, failed to excite Hiccup as it might have done in other circumstances.

They walked round and round in circles for about an hour and a half, looking for a way out, before realizing that there wasn't one. They sat down.

Without his Tribe around him, and facing Death, Alvin seemed to have returned to his old, pleasant self again. He even apologized for getting them into this mess.

"I just cannot believe this," moaned Fishlegs, shivering violently. "It's like some sort of NIGHT-MARE. I keep thinking we're safe, and then it seems that, NO, we're in some OTHER life-threatening situation even worse than the one we've just got away from."

"Okay," admitted Hiccup, trying to keep them from despairing, "it doesn't look good, but I'm sure I can think of a way out of here. . . ."

Toothless was sniffing away at the back of
the cavern, and he interrupted, calling out, "Toothless
can smell something m-metal over h-h-here!"

"Very clever, Toothless," said Hiccup, "but the
Treasure Hunt is over now."

"I mean," continued Fishlegs, "so far today we
have narrowly escaped being **1.** Torn to pieces by
Skullions. **2.** Eaten by Cannibal Outcasts. **3.** Burned
to death on board ship. **4.** Drowned at the bottom
of the ocean. . . . And now here we are, trapped in an
inaccessible underground cavern facing DEATH BY
SLOW STARVATION. . . . It's just been a REALLY
BAD day."

"N-n-not metal after all," Toothless called back
in disappointment. "It's just a d-d-door. . . ."

"A DOOR??" Alvin, Hiccup and Fishlegs
scrambled up and over towards Toothless, with
a sudden surge of hope.

Once they had scrabbled away at all the dust
and earth covering it, they found it *was* a door.
It was surprising they hadn't noticed it before.

"Is it a way out?" gasped Fishlegs.

"Not necessarily," Hiccup replied slowly.

A door with a DEATH'S HEAD painted on it.

A door with lettering on it that was horribly familiar to Hiccup.

Large, scrawling letters gouged out of the surface of the wood, probably with a sword.

"**DO NOT OPEN THIS DOOR**," it said, "**UNLESS YOU ARE THE TRUE HEIR TO GRIMBEARD THE GHASTLY. I REALLY MEAN IT THIS TIME, DEATH AND DESTRUCTION AND OTHER TRULY AWFUL THINGS WILL FOLLOW IF YOU OPEN THIS DOOR. THIS IS A PIRATE'S PRIVATE PERSONAL PROPERTY.**"

Hiccup looked straight into the suddenly glittering eyes of Alvin the Treacherous. All the pleasantness had fallen away from him again. He raised his arm with the Stormblade fixed into it.

Alvin didn't need to say anything.

Hiccup knew what he wanted.

"Ohhhhh no," said Hiccup, backing slowly away, "I'm not going to open this door."

"Oh, but you *are,*" smiled Alvin the Treacherous, resting the point of the Stormblade right in the center of Hiccup's chest.

"But I'm not the Heir to Grimbeard the Ghastly," Hiccup protested. "Snotlout is the Heir.

He's the one who found the treasure, remember the riddle?"

"Ah, but was that the *real* treasure that Snotlout found?" asked Alvin. "Perhaps Grimbeard put it there as a decoy, to make people think they'd found the real treasure, when all along it was lying here. What better hiding place than a cavern accessible only by water? And if that wasn't the real treasure, that means Snotlout isn't necessarily the True Heir to the Hairy Hooligans."

you
are the Heir
to
Grimbeard
the
Ghastly

"Well, that's a relief, in any case," said Fishlegs, trying to lighten the tension.

"YOU are the True Heir," said Alvin quietly. "When I asked on the *Lucky Thirteen* who was the Heir to the Hairy Hooligans, who stood up? YOU did. Not Snotlout. This has all been a Test, set by Grimbeard the Ghastly and Fate herself. Only now does the riddle make sense. For what have we just escaped from, but a watery grave?"

"And WHOSE Beast has just sniffed out this door? YOUR Beast."

"S-s-see?" said Toothless. "Toothless is better s-s-sniffer than Fireworm."

"YOU are the True Heir to the Hairy Hooligans, Hiccup," said Alvin. "And so only YOU can open this door and live."

"But I don't want to open this door," said Hiccup. "If you give me enough time I'm sure I can get us out of here without opening it. What about the booby traps? *You* open Grimbeard's coffin and you lose your right hand. . . . *We* open Grimbeard's treasure chest and it triggers a smell that wakes up the Skullions. . . . I KNOW that if we open this door something REALLY UNPLEASANT is going to

165

happen, sure as fish eggs are fish eggs. And the surprises are getting WORSE, if anything."

"I forgot to mention," said Alvin silkily, "if you don't open the door, you DIE."

He pressed the Stormblade forward a bit so that it pierced the skin just above Hiccup's heart.

"Let me get this straight," said Hiccup, "if I do open this door, you WON'T kill me or my friends?"

"I promise," said Alvin, "word of a Treacherous."

"Word of a Treacherous . . . ," groaned Fishlegs. "It says it all really. . . . He'll kill us as soon as he has the treasure . . . if there is any treasure behind that door. . . ."

"But otherwise he's going to kill us now," Hiccup pointed out. "I haven't got a lot of choice."

Hiccup leaned forward, biting his lip, and slid the heavy iron bolt to the left.

"NOT a good idea, NOT a good idea, NOT A GOOD IDEA," repeated Fishlegs and Toothless to themselves, closing their eyes.

Hiccup slow-ly opened the door. . . .

cr-e-e-e-e-e-e-e-e-e-e-e-e-e-e-a-k. . .

Alvin, Fishlegs, Hiccup and Toothless stood there, their mouths flopping open and shut like fish in their astonishment.

The door had opened on to another GIGANTIC cavern. This was filled to the brim with more treasure than you could possibly imagine in your wildest dreams, even were you as greedy as Alvin himself.

So indescribably beautiful was this treasure that it drew them into the room like a magnet.

It was all piled up on top of itself in crazy giant mountains. Mound after mound of golden coins with Caesar stamped on one side and Neptune on the other. Heap after heap of rubies fat and ripe as scallops and emeralds green as a mermaid's eye. Gorgeous silver cups with seahorses galloping delicately around them and golden necklaces as plump as oysters and swords as sharp as a conger's tooth with octopus tentacles winding themselves around the hilt.

It was the sort of treasure you could get lost in, and forget yourself and your mind and this world at all.

"Oh my," breathed Alvin the Treacherous, stepping forward. "Oh my, my, my . . ." And he reached out to grasp a cup, a glorious golden goblet, perfectly

168

round in shape, with dolphins playing around the rim, so beautifully carved that it looked as if they were alive and leaping in a miniature golden sea.

Toothless, Hiccup and Fishlegs recollected where they were, and slowly backed towards the open door while Alvin was so preoccupied.

But Alvin caught a glimpse of them out of the corner of his eye, and he stretched out and shut the door with the point of the Stormblade.

"Nobody leaves the cavern without asking Alvin," he said.

"Now, Alvin," said Hiccup nervously, "remember your promise. If I opened the door, you said you'd let us all live."

"Ye-e-e-e-s-s-s," said Alvin, considering the cup again, and then dropping it softly back on the pile. "The thing is, Outcasts don't always keep promises to other people. I blame our upbringing. My mother never really loved me, you know. But I always keep promises I make to MYSELF. And long ago, when that coffin lid snapped down and chopped off my hand, I made myself a very solemn promise indeed."

Alvin's pleasant eyes narrowed, and he sidled towards Hiccup like a predatory crab. "It's not that

I dislike you personally, Hiccup, but I swore to myself," said Alvin, still smiling, "that I would FIND Grimbeard's precious Treasure, and I would KILL his precious Heir. That's fair, isn't it, an Heir in exchange for a hand?"

And he made a vicious swipe at Hiccup with the Stormblade.

Hiccup dodged out of the way in the nick of time. He leapt nimbly onto the nearest mound of treasure and started scrambling up it.

"And with Grimbeard's own precious sword, too," chuckled Alvin. "Isn't fate ARTISTIC?"

"TOOTHLESS!" yelled Hiccup. "Get me a SWORD!"

Alvin climbed after him and made another wild lunge at his head.

Hiccup ducked behind a large golden chariot wheel.

"TOOTH-LESS!" cried Hiccup. "HURRY UP!"

"Okay, okay," muttered Toothless, who had flown to a pile of weaponry not far away. "K-k-keep your helmet on. T-t-toothless doing his BEST."

Toothless tried to pick up three of the swords, all of them as big and beautiful and flashy as the Stormblade itself. But they were all too heavy.

So he turned to something smaller, an undistinguished but serviceable object, a bit rusty at the edges perhaps. He could lift it easily with both talons, and flew with it to where Hiccup was climbing. He was a quarter of the way up a hill of treasure, hotly pursued by Alvin, who had little red lights dancing in his narrowed eyes and was swishing that Stormblade like he was a human flail.

Toothless to the rescue!

Toothless dropped the rusty sword into Hiccup's hand, and he caught it just in time to parry a blow by Alvin so terrible that if it had actually connected with Hiccup's neck, it might have removed his head from his shoulders then and there.

Hiccup caught the sword in his LEFT hand, because, if you remember, his right arm was dislocated and in a sling.

"This isn't going to last long," he thought to himself. It was a case of Man against Boy, and Hiccup wasn't exactly the greatest swordfighter in the Inner Isles even with his *right* hand.

"Keep your point UP, Hiccup," shouted Fishlegs, desperately trying to clamber up after them so he could help. "Eye on the swords at all times, a strong wrist, remember your footwork. . . ."

Alvin the Treacherous gave a great swipe at Hiccup's belly, and Hiccup was surprised to find his left arm jerk up and his own sword block Alvin's in the nick of time.

Alvin was equally surprised, and he hauled his great sword over his wicked head and he brought it down towards Hiccup's neck, and Hiccup's arm flashed up and parried the blow just before it bit.

Astonished, Alvin began raining blows thick and fast, swiping and slashing and lunging, and Hiccup's left arm parried every thrust as if it had a life of its own.

"Well, suffering swordfish," exclaimed Fishlegs. "Hiccup is LEFT-HANDED."

I would not have you think that this was a fight that Hiccup would be proud to look back upon NOW. For Hiccup would grow up to be a Master Swordsman, a Genius of the Art, and this fight, by comparison with the extraordinary skill with which he fought later, was clumsy work, mostly defensive strokes.

And although I would love to say that Alvin the Treacherous was a brilliant swordfighter, the truth is that he was just so-so at the Art, preferring to poison his enemy's cup or bash him from behind with a rock to fighting him face to face.

But he was still much older, stronger and more experienced than Hiccup.

And while it might not have been the best fight Hiccup ever fought, it was certainly the one he would look back on with the most astonishment and pride.

For it was the first time in his life that Hiccup realized he was left-handed.

Imagine if you had spent the whole first part of your life trying to walk on your hands. The clumsiness of it, always falling over, always stumbling, always the last at everything. Imagine the joy of discovering that in fact you could walk on your feet after all.

That is what it felt like to Hiccup fighting with his left hand for the first time. So exhilarating was the feeling that he was even starting to enjoy himself.

Hiccup was helped by Toothless, who swooped down and attacked Alvin's head so that Alvin was constantly distracted.

"Unfair," smiled Alvin. "I never thought Grimbeard's Heir would stoop to TWO AGAINST ONE."

The excitement made Hiccup overconfident and so he called out, "Leave him to me, Toothless!"

"Leave him to you?" Fishlegs shouted up furiously. "What do you mean, LEAVE HIM TO YOU??? CARRY ON, TOOTHLESS, AND THAT IS AN ORDER! This is REAL LIFE, Hiccup, not a Swordfighting at Sea lesson, and you need all the help you can get. . . ."

In fact, the practice from the Sword-fighting at Sea lessons were a big help to Hiccup.

HOW TO SWORDFIGHT

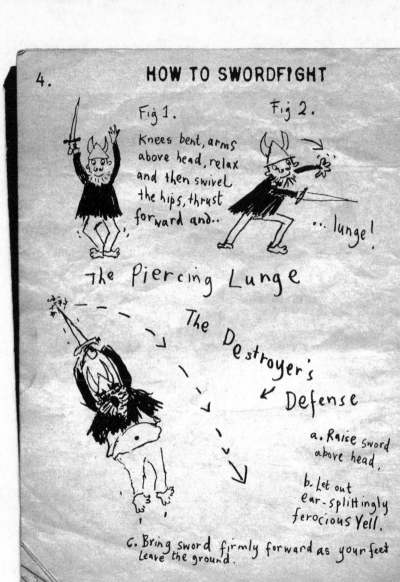

Fig 1.

Knees bent, arms above head, relax and then swivel the hips, thrust forward and...

Fig 2.

... lunge!

The Piercing Lunge

The Destroyer's Defense

a. Raise sword above head.

b. Let out ear-splittingly ferocious yell.

c. Bring sword firmly forward as your feet leave the ground.

The Fighting-Against-Superior-Numbers-Maneuver

Remember to keep your weight on the back foot at all times. Be careful not to remove your own head with that axe.

The Confusing-the-enemy—Bottoms-Up-Routine

Only for the very confident.

The shifting, moving ground of the treasure mound was rather similar to the movement of the deck at sea. Hiccup kept his balance more easily than Alvin, who continually staggered and lost his footing.

Nonetheless, it was soon clear that although Hiccup was enjoying himself, he wasn't winning the fight, even with Toothless's help. With a grim smile on his lips, Alvin the Treacherous fought Hiccup back and back, eyes aglow with that red light, back to his old smooth self again.

"Come on, Hiccup," he wheedled, "don't be scared of your old pal, Treacherous. I wouldn't harm a hair" *(swipe)* "on your head" *(swipe)*.

"Listen, Alvin," urged Hiccup, as he parried each blow, "I'm sure we can all get away safely if you forget about the treasure. . . ."

"Oh, I will," promised Alvin, "just as soon as I've killed you, I will."

"Look, Alvin," reasoned Hiccup, "it's never too late to change. You've still got a chance to live life differently, make friends, start a family. . . ."

"Stop it," said Alvin, "you're making me laugh. *You* give *me* a second chance? That's really funny, that is. You're a heartbeat away from the abyss,

178

a mere child fighting a fully grown man, and *you're* giving *me* second chances? It's too kind of you." He made a particularly violent lunge that Hiccup just managed to dodge, and very nearly lost his balance doing so.

"It's too late for me," laughed Alvin. "I'm rotten to the core and I like being rotten. The treasure has got me and I like being got." He raised his sword way above his head as Hiccup clutched desperately at the shifting coins to steady himself.

"But I appreciate your concern," said Alvin, bringing the sword down with such savage force that it would have cut Hiccup in half — if he had not spotted it coming and made one last leap out of the way.

So that the blow, instead of separating Hiccup into two pieces, caught Alvin completely off balance, and he stepped back onto the treasure mound behind, one on which they had not fought before . . .

. . . and the treasure unexpectedly reared up beneath him, as if it were alive.

18. GRIMBEARD THE GHASTLY'S FINAL SURPRISE

The entire mound reared up and shook itself, cups and jewels and swords and coins cascading down the sides like molten lava.

And something that looked like a big white rope reached out of the treasure and wound its way around Alvin's waist.

It wasn't a rope.

It was a singularly unattractive white tentacle that looked as if it were made out of a quivering piece of fat. The tentacle was dotted with small indentations out of which there oozed a disgusting whitey-gray sticky sludge that smelt indescribably awful.

Alvin shrieked in horror as the treasure dropped away to reveal the creature that had been sleeping underneath it, a creature they had awoken with their swordfight.

It was Grimbeard the Ghastly's last surprise, his FINAL booby trap.

He had left it there to guard the treasure, a monster that Hiccup had heard of in Legends,

but never seen before, and one that he sincerely hoped he would never, ever have to see again.

It was the same animal that surprised the little lost Deadly Nadder, the day before, if you remember, and it was called a Monstrous Strangulator.

A Strangulator was a gigantic Monster genetically related to dragons, octopuses and snakes. It had tiny withered dragon wings and tiny crippled dragon legs that were basically useless, as it heaved its great body through underground tunnels like a serpent, leaving a trail of gooey slime.

It had never seen daylight and was the color of nothing. Its tentacles had obviously found a way up through to the upper caves of the Wild Dragon Cliffs, for it was transparent, and you could actually see the forms of unfortunate dragons it had eaten moving through its digestive system. Some, further down the Strangulator's great length, were lying quite still. Others that he had eaten more recently were jerking about, and one was trying to fly, trapped in the Monster's great throat.

The naturalist in Hiccup automatically identified the species — Monstrous Nightmare, Deadly Nadder, Common or Garden times three — making their slow

progress through the
Serpent's alimentary canal.

So small was the
Creature's brain in proportion to its
size that it had difficulty in keeping sensory track of all of its squirming tentacles, and they
wandered about as if they had independent lives of
their own. The Creature had to concentrate hard to
make the tentacle that was holding Alvin move very
slowly up to its head so it could have a look at him,
unsure of what to make of this weird new animal.

"Isss food?" hissed the Serpent musingly to itself.

Hiccup practically cried with relief. For the
creature was speaking a dialect of Dragonese, a very
ancient form of it, but Dragonese nonetheless.

And Hiccup was of the opinion that if you could
talk to your killer, you were in with a chance.

Alvin struggled wildly and slashed at the great
squeezing tentacle with the Stormblade.

"Tickle me with your prickle, would you?" said
the Creature. *"Then I'll tickle you with mine. . . ."*

And languidly, it dangled the tip of its tail in
front of Alvin's face.

Hiccup had seen such a tail on much smaller

18{

animals. It was filled to the tip with a grass-green venom, pure as glass. There was a plunger a little way down, and the tip just had to penetrate its victim, the plunger go down, and it was goodnight sweet world, hello Valhalla.

"Oh *excellent,*" thought Hiccup to himself. "A *poisonous* Monstrous Strangulator. My favorite kind."

Alvin fainted as soon as he set eyes on that deadly tail. He was frightened of needles.

So the Strangulator didn't even bother to inject him. It just swallowed him whole, alive, just as he was, Stormblade and all.

In fascinated horror, Hiccup watched the now awake and struggling form of Alvin traveling down the Strangulator's transparent throat.

"So," thought Hiccup, "the Eater of Human Flesh is eaten himself. Isn't fate artistic?"

Sometimes it is harder to force yourself to stand still than it is to run away, but Hiccup knew that he wouldn't have a chance if he tried to escape. This animal was just too big. So Hiccup froze, in the hope that the Creature's eyesight was poor, like other beasts that lived solely underground.

Hiccup was probably right, but one of those

constantly moving tentacles accidentally bumped into him, and as soon as it made contact with his warm body it automatically wrapped itself around Hiccup, and lifted him into the air.

"A Plan!" Fishlegs shouted out wildly from below. "You need a Fiendishly Clever Plan!"

"Thank you, Fishlegs," said Hiccup, his mind flicking about like a shrimp in a net, and trying to ignore the terrible squeezing around his chest. "I'm aware of that . . . TOOTHLESS! Come up here!"

The tentacles were turning Hiccup over and over. Toothless flapped up, and hovered as close as he could. Hiccup shouted something into the little dragon's ear.

"That's a t-t-t-terrible plan," moaned Toothless, shaking his head.

"Just do as you're told for ONCE in your life," yelled Hiccup.

While the Creature remained unconscious of having caught anything, Hiccup still stood a chance of escape. With his sword, he jabbed away at the sticky tentacle that was encircling his trunk and it seemed to be loosening. . . .

Way down at the bottom of the treasure mound, Fishlegs was frantically trying to be helpful.

In front of him, there lay a heavily bejeweled monstrosity of a sword. Despite the fact that it was nearly as big as himself, Fishlegs managed to pick it up from the floor. Purple in the face with the extraordinary effort, he lifted it high, high above his head, ready to launch it at the Creature's stomach. . . .

he
lifted
the sword
high, high
above his head...

186

Unfortunately the backwards momentum of the sword was so great that Fishlegs toppled ve-ry slowly backwards with it. There was a bronze shield on the floor behind him, and he landed on it with such force that he knocked himself out.

The noise of Fishlegs's head connecting with the shield caught the Creature's attention and light finally dawned in its dull eyes, which swam into focus on Hiccup. Its tentacles gripped strongly and escape became impossible.

"More food?" it mused to itself.

"NOT food!" Hiccup shouted out. "I'm POISONOUS. Very, very POISONOUS!"

"Poissonousssssss?" hissed the Creature. *"It ssspeakss and iss poisssonousss, is it? I'M poissssson-oussssss. Ssssssssee?"*

And it waved the deadly plunger of its tail menacingly in front of Hiccup.

"Don't like it when the food ssssspeaks . . . ," whined the Creature to itself. *"Isss trichsssssy when it sssspeaks . . . kill it quickly before it trichsssss me. . . ."*

It wrapped its tentacles a little tighter around Hiccup in order to suffocate him.

"This is all very interesting," Hiccup managed to choke out, his eyes popping. "So, how were you thinking of killing me, exactly?"

Gradually, the awful pressure on Hiccup's chest eased as the Strangulator considered this question.

"Well," it said slowly, *"I wasssss thinking of sssssssqueezing you to death. . . ."*

"I only ask," said Hiccup, gasping for air, "because I was recently nearly swallowed by a Seadragonus Giganticus Maximus, who said that you Undergrounders were very primitive animals, poorly armed, and only capable of basic forms of killing, such as strangulation."

The Creature stopped squeezing entirely.

"That'ssss very rude," it hissed eventually, rather hurt. *"What isssss thissss Giganti-Maxi-thingy anyway?"*

"Release your tentacles a bit," said Hiccup, "and I'll tell you."

"Okay," said the Strangulator, *"but no trickssssing or I'll get crosssssss."*

Slowly the Creature unwound its tentacles, leaving them only loosely wrapped about the boy. Hiccup took in great relieved gulps of air.

"A Seadragonus Giganticus Maximus," Hiccup

continued, "is a gigantic, scary killing machine as big as a mountain...."

"*I'm big* . . . ," the Creature pointed out.

"It has at least three ways of killing," said Hiccup. "It can rip you to pieces with its talons, bite you to bits with its teeth or fry you to a frazzle with its fire."

"*I can do that* . . . ," said the Creature, less certainly.

"No, you can't," said Hiccup. "You haven't got any talons, teeth or fire."

"*Ssssso I haven't,*" said the Strangulator, very disappointed. "*But I can sssssssqueeze you to death*. . . ." He brightened up and began to wrap his tentacles around Hiccup again.

"So OLD-FASHIONED!" shrieked Hiccup hurriedly. "What about the POISON? That's the most modern method of killing around. A Seadragonus Giganticus Maximus hasn't got any poison...."

"*Hasssssssn't it?*" asked the Creature delightedly.

"No, it hasn't," said Hiccup. "I'm very curious to see how one of these fancy new poisons works."

"*It'sssss not a niccccce way to go,*" warned the Creature.

189

It pointed the sharp needle of its tail straight at Hiccup's heart.

Suddenly, Toothless flew into the Strangulator's field of vison. The Creature lost concentration for a second as the little dragon zoomed up and down right in front of its eyes. By the time it had coordinated its tentacles enough to frighten Toothless away, the Strangulator was very, very cross.

"I told you, no trickssssssing!" it hissed, with venom in its voice. *"Thisssss will shut you up. . . ."*

Fishlegs came back into consciousness just in time to see the Strangulator inject the whole tail's-worth of green poison, enough to kill the entire population of Rome, into the flesh beneath Hiccup's shirt.

19. THE HEIR TO GRIMBEARD THE GHASTLY

"So," chatted Hiccup, "while we're waiting for this poison to take effect, why don't you tell me how it works?"

"*Well,*" crowed the Strangulator, "*you will lose control of your tentaclesss ass they ssstart to ssssstiffen. . . .*"

"I can feel a sort of tingling in my feet, like pins and needles," admitted Hiccup.

The Strangulator's own tentacles were leaping about wildly, as stiff as boards.

"*The poissson turnsss sssome victimsss green before they die . . . ,*" hissed the Strangulator gleefully.

"Is it just me," said Hiccup, "or is there a sort of greenish tinge to my left arm?"

There wasn't. It was as white and freckled as ever.

But a strange green cloud was building within the Strangulator's transparent body, gradually obscuring the unfortunate dragons he was digesting.

"*. . . and then as the poissson reaches the head,*"

continued the Strangulator, *"**the nervoussss ssyssstem sssssimply explodesss. . . ."***

He looked at Hiccup hopefully. Nothing seemed to be happening.

*"**That'sss funny,**"* said the Strangulator. *"**It doesn't sssseem to be working. . . ."***

"Maybe some people take longer," said Hiccup reassuringly. "You're looking a little peaked yourself, maybe you should lie down."

The Strangulator looked down at itself. The green cloud had now blown into every crook and cranny of its body, and was finally approaching its tiny brain. . . .

"AAAAAAAAAAAAAAAAAAAAAGH!"

screeched the Strangulator.

The nervous system of the Strangulator simply exploded.

All of its electric circuits lit up like lightbulbs. It thrashed around like a mad thing, knocking out great chunks of rock from the sides of the cave and sending treasure flying through the air in all directions.

Fishlegs hid himself underneath an overhanging

rock in order not to be hit by the whirling coils. Toothless crawled into a crevice in the ceiling. For about a minute and a half the Strangulator threw itself wildly off the walls of the cavern, screeching a strange primeval agonized shriek. Then all of its tentacles stood out straight and stiff and it fell to the ground.

The Strangulator jerked a few more times in agony. Its tail with the dangerous tip lashed ferociously for a moment or two. And then all was silence in the Great Cavern. Huge clouds of dust gradually dispersed.

Fishlegs crawled out of his hiding place.

He scrambled over slimy rockfalls, slimy treasure and even slimier coils of Strangulator, looking for Hiccup.

Hiccup was dazed but alive. He'd had a tidal wave of a ride, thrown this way and that way until his teeth rattled. But the great coils of the tentacle wrapped around his body had cushioned him from any hurt.

He beamed at Fishlegs and Toothless.

"That was one STUPID Monster," he said.

"How did you DO it? How did you DO it?" asked Fishlegs again and again in amazement as he and Toothless unwound the tentacle from Hiccup's body.

For answer, Hiccup lifted up his shirt, and there, wrapped around his chest, was the very tip of the tentacle . . . and in the gelatinous transparent flesh of it was a giant needle puncture mark, with the green poison clearly visible coursing underneath the skin.

What Hiccup had done was to pull his shirt OVER the end of the tentacle while Toothless was distracting the Creature. The Strangulator had so lost sensory contact with the ends of its tentacles that it did not realize that it was in fact injecting ITSELF under the white material of Hiccup's shirt.

"That particular plan," said Fishlegs at last, "required a Fiendish Amount of LUCK."

"It WAS lucky," admitted Hiccup happily, "but we're ALIVE, aren't we?"

Fishlegs grinned back at him and Toothless did three back somersaults in the air and a congratulatory cock-a-doodle-doo.

"And that swordfighting. Where did THAT come from? You've always been grim at swordfighting."

"Swapped hands," mumbled Hiccup, beaming but a bit embarrassed.

196

"A left-handed genius who single-handedly defeated Alvin the Treacherous AND a Monstrous Strangulator," gloated Fishlegs. "This is going to look so GOOD when we tell everybody back home. I just can't WAIT to see the look on Snotlout's face when he sets eyes on this treasure. It makes that poxy little box he dug up on the Isle of the Skullions look pretty measly."

"Yeeees," said Hiccup slowly. "But we ARE still trapped in an inaccessible underground cavern, aren't we? We have to GET OUT OF HERE first."

Fishlegs's face fell. "So we do," he admitted. "But the Creature must have some way from this cavern up to the caves in the Wild Dragon Cliff. . . . I mean, look at those dragons in his digestive system, he must have been feeding off the Dragon Nursery for years. All we have to do is go through these Caliban Caves and —"

"N-n-no," said Toothless firmly. "T-t-toothless knows. Toothless grow up here. Other C-c-creatures in there much bigger and b-b-badder than that one. . . ."

"Okay then," said Hiccup. "We go back the way we came. Let's hope that door still opens."

The door did still open.

As they were opening it, Hiccup noticed a piece of paper nailed on their side of it.

It was a letter.

It was written in the same scrawly handwriting as Grimbeard's riddle, and it was addressed to the **"TRUE HEIR OF GRIMBEARD THE GHASTLY."**

Hiccup took the letter off the nail and read it.

"Maybe Grimbeard the Ghastly wasn't so bad after all . . . ," said Hiccup slowly.

"There you are," said Fishlegs, who was reading

over Hiccup's shoulder. "He said it was YOUR treasure, to do as you liked with."

Hiccup sighed. He thought of the greedy look in Stoick's eyes when he held the Stormblade. He thought of Baggybum and Stoick arguing over the treasure chest.

"Yes," said Hiccup, "and I DO know what to do with it."

He picked up a piece of charcoal from the cavern floor, wrote some words on the bottom of the letter, and pinned it back on the door.

"STILL . . . NOT . . . READY . . . ," read Fishlegs.

Fishlegs hurried after Hiccup, who was now looking at the cavern's exit hole to the sea, thinking hard.

"What do you mean, *still not ready*?" demanded Fishlegs.

"I mean," said Hiccup, "that the treasure is staying right here. That this is our SECRET and we tell NOBODY. If we get out of here alive, we just say we washed up on the shore a couple of beaches down, no mention of the existence of this cavern, nothing."

"You CANNOT BE SERIOUS," said Fishlegs. "We could be HEROES here, and besides, if we don't tell everybody what happened, they'll all go on thinking that Snotlout is the True Heir to the Hairy Hooligans."

DEAR HEIR,

(said the letter)

I have had a glorious Viking life. But now that I am an old, old man I find I am not so happy with my fifty years of rollicking and robbery, fighting and fresh air. I wonder if I might have run things differently. This treasure, for instance. The Sagas will tell you that the stealing of it was my **Most Magnificent Moment.** But since then, it has been tearing my once-happy band of burglars apart with **GREED** and **LUST FOR POWER.** We are just not ready to look after this treasure. So I have decided to get rid of it.

I know that there will be men who will hear of the Legend of the Treasure and come looking for it, and for them I have buried a small chest on the Isle of the Skullions as a decoy, so that they will think that the hunt ends there. I have hidden the

REAL TREASURE

deep, deep in this underground cavern. It has taken many many months for my dragons to swim down here with it. It is guarded by water one way

and the Caliban Caves the other. I have placed
an infant Strangulator in the Cavern who shall
grow in time to be a terrible Guardian indeed.
I dream of a time in the future when men will be
able to own such beautiful and dangerous
things and use them wisely.

I dream of an Heir who shall be a Dragon-
Whisperer, a Swordfighter, a Man who talks with
Monsters and who will harness the power of Thor's
thunder itself.... This Heir will come and he will
find my treasure. I give it to him freely, all of it,
and he shall know what to do with it.

I wish you good luck and a nice strong wind,

Grimbeard the Ghastly

P.S. I hope you have a dragon
with you, he can help you to the
surface. Otherwise I am afraid
you are done for.

Hiccup looked miserable. "I guess that's right," he said. "But then if I really *am* the True Heir, I have to do what I think is the right thing for the Tribe, don't I? And this is definitely the right thing. That treasure is Bad Trouble."

Hiccup would not change his mind.

"Let's just concentrate on getting back home," he said.

It took Hiccup two or three hours of hard thinking to work out how to use one dragon to get himself and Fishlegs up through hundreds of feet of water and back to the surface without drowning.

The solution is quite simple, if you ever find yourself in a similarly tricky situation.

A dragon's breath, even when it exhales, is composed almost entirely of pure oxygen. It is this that makes it so very flammable. All they needed to do was to rise to the surface (slowly, so as not to get the bends) with Toothless swimming beside them and occasionally blowing into their noses when they ran out of breath.

A dragon never runs out of breath because just below its horns it has a fully working set of gills. As soon as it enters the sea it can shut off its lungs and get its oxygen from the water rather than the air.

Hiccup and Fishlegs resurfaced after about ten minutes. There was plenty of debris floating around, because they were not far from where the *Lucky Thirteen* had made its final journey to the bottom of the ocean. The boys each got hold of one end of an oar, and steered their way around the corner to where there was a beach to land on.

Fishlegs tried to persuade Hiccup to change his mind all the way home.

At last he said in exasperation, "You're NEVER going to be a Hero with this attitude. How *can* you be with no one to cheer, no one to clap?"

"Okay then," Hiccup sighed. "I'll never be a Hero. All I know is that I'm supposed to be the

Future Leader of this Tribe and I want there to be a Tribe left to lead. And that seems more important to me than being a Hero."

They staggered through the heather towards the Hooligan Village, which was strangely silent and deserted. No smoke curled from the rooftops, no children quarreled in the streets, no dragons were fighting in the thatch.

"Please, please, good god Woden," prayed Hiccup, "PLEASE let everybody be alive."

Everybody *was* alive.

Miraculously, no one had drowned during the sinking of the *Lucky Thirteen*.

The Hooligans sailed the heavily overloaded *Hammerhead* back to Berk, with the Outcasts tied up as their prisoners.

With typical generosity, they set the Outcasts free.

I fear the Outcasts were not as grateful as they should have been, and this would not be the last the Hooligans would see of these vicious people. For the moment, however, they returned to the Outcast Lands humiliated, unarmed and with a hunger for revenge.

The Hooligans were not in much better shape themselves. They were a hardy race, and drowning was

an occupational hazard, but the loss of the only son of
the Chief was a big blow, whether he was the Heir or not.

Stoick sat for an hour at the edge of the sea.
As soon as Snotlout's treasure had disappeared
beneath the waves it had lost its magic for him.
He kept on seeing in his mind's eye his son, Hiccup,
standing on the deck of the *Lucky Thirteen,* saying,
"I AM THE HEIR TO STOICK THE VAST."

He tore out his golden earrings, and threw
them into the ocean. And then he went home and
sat in front of his shrine to Woden.

So this was why, when Fishlegs, Hiccup and
Toothless came stumbling and limping into the
Hooligan Village, everyone had locked themselves
indoors, the shutters were shut up, doors were closed,
fires were unlit.

It was only a chance that the wooden window
had blown open in Gobber the Belch's home. He went
to close it, and happened to spot the bedraggled
friends lurching along. . . . And then he let out a great
bellow of, "They're ALIVE!!!"

The shout went from house to house like
watch fires lighting from hill to hill, and the Hairy
Hooligans rushed out of their front doors like a crowd

of jubilant sea elephants, and they swooped on the three companions and lifted them onto their muscly shoulders with great happy shouts of, "They're ALIVE! They're ALIVE! THEY'RE ALIVE! THEY'RE ALIVE!"

Snotlout was already furious to find that people had been more concerned about mourning Hiccup and Fishlegs than congratulating HIM on being the Hero of the Hour on the Isle of the Skullions.

Imagine how cross he was to run out of his house in curiosity at the commotion, to find himself barged out of the way by Gobber the Belch and Nobber Nobrains, and practically trampled into the ground by a clapping mob carrying Hiccup shoulder-high through the Village.

Hiccup, who was quite clearly, yet again, NOT dead, NOT drowned, NOT safely out of the way.

The happy Hooligans reached the door of their Chieftain's house and banged on it, crying, "Open up, open up, they're alive, they're alive!"

Stoick the Vast lifted his great hairy head as if he was dreaming, staggered to the door, and there, on the doorstep, was HIS SON, Hiccup.

Stoick the Vast, Terror of the Seas, Most

High Ruler of the Hairy Hooligans, O Hear His
Name and Tremble, Ugh, Ugh, picked up his son and
hugged him, while the crowd cheered and cheered.
And that was how Toothless found and lost a
marvelous treasure all in the space of an afternoon . . .

. . . And how Hiccup finally got himself a sword
and learnt how to use it . . .

. . . And how Fishlegs discovered that you don't
always have to be a Hero to get a Hero's Welcome.

EPILOGUE

A few months afterwards, I had a dream.

It was a dream about shipwrecks, perhaps because I had been doing a lot of that lately. The ship was called the *Endless Journey,* and just before it disappeared beneath the waves, the ferocious looking captain, who had a strange smile on his face, threw a sword up, up into the air. It spun end to end over the waves, through the atmosphere and into space and stars and never-ending time, where, to my surprise, my own left hand sprang out of its own accord and caught it.

As soon as I awoke, I got up and brought out that uninspiring sword that Toothless had picked for me in the cavern of the Treasure, the one with which I had fought Alvin the Treacherous. I turned it over and over, and inspected the dull little object for quite half an hour. And eventually I found that by twisting and twisting it, the knob at the end fell off and there was a small piece of paper rolled up in a little hollowed-out compartment inside. A small fragment of paper on which was written the following words:

The Last Will and Testament
~of~
Grimbeard the Ghastly

I leave to my True Heir,
this my favorite sword.
  Because the Stormblade
  always lunged a little to
  the left.
And the Best is not always
the most Obvious.

  Yours,
  In the hope that
  you will make a better
  Leader than
  I was,

G.G.

Now I am an old, old man, the same age as Grimbeard the Ghastly when he got his dragons to swim down to the cavern with the treasure. Toothless and Fishlegs and I have kept the secret of what really happened on that terrible day all those years ago. . . .

But because I am writing my memoirs I find I have to write it down, as it is such an important part of my journey to becoming a Hero. Even though I know I will never be able to show it to anyone of my own time.

As soon as I have finished writing these papers, I shall lock them in a box. I shall throw that box into the sea.

And I shall throw it hoping, like Grimbeard the Ghastly, that someday it may be found by someone who will be a better Leader than I have been.

Someone living way, way in the future, in times more civilized than those in which I have lived, where men can own beautiful and dangerous things and use them wisely.

Surely that would be the last Hiccup would see of that wicked villain, **Alvin the Treacherous?**

His grim hook sank to the bottom of the ocean with the wreck of the Lucky Thirteen. *He himself was last seen struggling in the throat of a Monstrous Strangulator in an inaccessible cavern deep, deep underground. . . .*

Nobody could get out of that situation alive . . .

Or could they???

Look out for the next volume of Hiccup's memoirs. . . .

Don't miss Hiccup's next adventure!

HOW TO TRAiN YOUR

DRAGON

Book 3

How to Speak Dragonese

1. THE BOARDING-AN-ENEMY-SHIP LESSON

Once upon a foggy day in a cold, cold country long, long ago, seven small Viking boats floated through the Sea-Known-as-Woden's-Bathtub. The fog had swallowed up the Peaceable Country to the north, and the Isle of Berk to the west, and, indeed, had swallowed up so much of everything that it was as if the boats were sky-boats, and had left the earth entirely, and were sailing through cloud banks way, way up in the air.

In the first boat, *The Fat Boar,* sat Gobber the Belch, a six-and-a-half-foot giant in teeny-weeny hairy shorts, who had leg muscles so enormous they had muscles of their own, and a beard like a hedgehog struck by lightning. Gobber was the teacher in charge of the Pirate Training Program on the Isle of Berk, and this sail through the fog was part of a Boarding-an-Enemy-Ship lesson.

The six boy-sized boats that were following *The Fat Boar* each had two boys in them, and these boys were Gobber's pupils, young members of the Tribe of the Hairy Hooligans.

"OK, YOU DISGUSTING GLOBS OF GIRLY SNOT!" yelled Gobber, in a bellow so loud it could be heard several miles away. "WE ARE NOW GOING TO PRACTICE BOARDING AN ENEMY SHIP ON THE EASY TARGET OF A PEACEABLE FISHING BOAT ... CAN ANYONE REMEMBER THE FIRST RULE OF AMBUSH?"

"TAKE THE ENEMY BY SURPRISE, SIR!" shouted out Snotface Snotlout, a tall, unpleasantly smug-looking boy with gigantic nostrils and the beginnings of a small mustache.

"Very good, Snotlout," purred Gobber the Belch, and he continued at full volume: "IN A FOG THIS THICK YOUR VICTIM SHIP WILL NOT HAVE A CHANCE OF SEEING YOU COMING!"

They can hear *us, though,* thought Hiccup Horrendous Haddock the Third, gloomily trying to peer through the fog, *unless, of course, we have the luck to stumble across some completely* deaf *Peaceable fishermen . . .*

Hiccup Horrendous Haddock the Third is, rather surprisingly, the Hero of this story. I say surprisingly, because the first thing you noticed about Hiccup was how very, very ordinary he was. He was on the small side, with a slightly freckled, absolutely average face that would always get overlooked in a crowd.

His dragon, Toothless, who was at that moment asleep down the front of Hiccup's shirt, was just as average as his owner. The only truly remarkable thing about Toothless was how remarkably *small* he was. He was at least half the size of the other boys' dragons.

And, as you can imagine, this wasn't something to boast about.

Gobber's shouting woke the little dragon up. He poked his nose out of the neck of Hiccup's tunic. "W-w-what's happening?" he asked sleepily in Dragonese.*

---

* Dragons spoke Dragonese. Only Hiccup could understand this fascinating language.

"Oh, nothing unusual," Hiccup whispered back, scratching Toothless behind the horns. (He loved that.) "Gobber is shouting, Snotlout is showing off, and we're all out here floating in the fog and the cold when we could be tucked up in front of a roasting fire . . . You can go back to sleep if you like."

Toothless chuckled. "You V-v-vikings are as m-m-mad as mackerel," he said. "W-w-wake Toothless up when it's l-l-lunchtime . . ." And he burrowed back down to the nice warm spot just next to Hiccup's left armpit and closed his eyes again.

Hiccup was sharing his boat with his best friend Fishlegs, who was even skinnier than Hiccup and looked a lot like a daddy longlegs with asthma and a squint. Fishlegs put his hand up in the air.

"It's all very well that they can't see us coming, sir," he pointed out logically, "but how are *we* going to see them so we can board *them* in the first place?"

"Easy-peasy, o plankton-brain," boomed Gobber, very pleased with himself. "Peaceable fishing boats are always followed by flocks of Lesser

Blackbacked Seadragons, hoping for a bite. All you
have to do is follow the racket they make and you'll
have found yourself a boat. You then simply board the
boat yelling the Hooligan War Cry: repeat after me . . .
YAAAAAAAAAH!" yelled Gobber the Belch.

"YAAAAAAAAAH!" yelled ten of the boys
back at him, brandishing their swords like maniacs.

"Yaaaaah," repeated Hiccup and Fishlegs,
without much enthusiasm.

"The Peaceables are terrified of us Hooligans, Woden only knows why . . . Right, lads — you steal one of their helmets to prove you have completed the exercise, and report back to me. **THIS IS GOING TO BE LIKE BURGLING BERRIES FROM A BABY!**" boomed Gobber the Belch.

"Oh, I nearly forgot. Silly me . . ." Gobber laughed carelessly. "The one thing you *do* have to bear in mind is that **ON NO ACCOUNT SHOULD YOU LEAVE THIS BAY.** This is **VERY IMPORTANT** because just to the south of here runs the Summer Current, a warm stream of water, and you all know what lives in the Summer Current . . ."

"Sharkworms," gulped Fishlegs.

"That's right, Fishlegs," boomed Gobber. "I know Hiccup, our natural history expert, can tell us something about Sharkworms."

"Certainly sir," replied Hiccup, delighted to be asked a question about his favorite subject, dragons. He took out of his pocket a small scruffy notebook with *How to Speak Dragonese* written in large scrawly letters on the front. In this book Hiccup kept notes on the Dragonese language and descriptions of the various species of dragons and their habits.

"Well," said Hiccup, having trouble reading his own handwriting, "Sharkworms are a kind of dragon that look a lot like sharks. The adults can grow to about six meters in length, they have at least five rows of teeth —"

"GET ON WITH IT, BOY!" yelled Gobber.

"They are highly carnivorous and they not only scavenge off ships but climb aboard and attack you there . . . On land they can easily outrun a man . . . I would suggest, sir, that if there was even a *chance* we could run into Sharkworms we should leave the area immediately."

"For Thor's sake, boy," grinned Gobber the Belch, "with that kind of attitude you might never leave the house. I'm training you to be *pirates,* not *softies*."

"What happens if we get lost, sir?" pleaded Fishlegs.

"Lost?" snorted Gobber. "LOST! Vikings don't get LOST!"

"Honestly, sir," sneered Snotface Snotlout, "I don't know why you don't throw Hiccup the Useless and his fishlegged failure of a friend out of the Tribe completely. They're a disgrace to all of us."

Hiccup and Fishlegs looked miserable.

"I mean look at their *boat,* sir," continued the sneering Snotlout. "We're *Vikings,* sir, the greatest shipbuilders the Ancient World has ever known, sir. A raft like that just makes us look ridiculous."

"You think you're so clever, Snotlout," retorted Hiccup determinedly, "but this boat can go a lot faster than you think. Looks aren't everything, you know . . ."

Unfortunately, Snotlout had a point.

The Hopeful Puffin was more of a floating accident than an actual boat.

She had been built by Hiccup and Fishlegs in Shipbuilding lessons, and they were both hopeless at woodwork. Something kept on going wrong with the design and instead of being long and thin like a Viking ship should be, she had ended up fat and almost completely round. Her mast was too long and leaned lopsidedly to the left, so that in a strong wind she went round in circles.

She also had a leak.

Every half an hour Fishlegs or Hiccup had to remember to bail out the seawater that had collected in the bottom of the boat with Hiccup's helmet (Fishlegs's helmet also had a leak).

Gobber the Belch looked at *The Hopeful Puffin.*

"Mmm," said Gobber thoughtfully. "You might have a point, Snotlout. NOW!" he continued briskly.

"At the sound of my horn, the exercise will begin."

He raised a curly-wurly bugle to his lips.

"Ooooh, jumping jellyfish," moaned Fishlegs, "I HATE the Pirate Training Program! We're going to get lost . . . We're going to sink . . . We're going to get eaten slowly by Sharkworms . . ."

"S-C-R-E-E-E-ECH!" screamed the bugle.

The Hopeful Puffin

Cressida Cowell
and
Lily AND BALOO

ABOUT THE AUTHOR

Cressida Cowell lives in London with her husband, Simon; their children, Maisie, Clementine, and Alexander; and two cats, Lily and Baloo. In addition to translating Hiccup's memoirs, she has also written and illustrated picture books including *How to Be a Viking*, *Little Bo Peep's Library Book*, and *That Rabbit Belongs to Emily Brown*. Her website is www.cressidacowell.co.uk.